SAVAGE ADORATION

SAVAGE
ADORATION

A Novel

Gale Zoë Garnett

Exile Editions

Publishers of singular
Fiction, Poetry, Drama, Nonfiction and Graphic Books

2009

Library and Archives Canada Cataloguing in Publication

Garnett, Gale Zoë, 1949—
Savage adoration / Gale Zoë Garnett

ISBN 978-1-55096-120-1

I. Title.

PS8563.A6732S29 2009   C813'.54   C2009-900965-X

Design and Composition by KellEn-K StyleSet
Typeset in Stone Serif, Big Caslon and Garamond fonts at the
 Moons of Jupiter Studios
Printed in Canada by Gauvin Imprimerie

The publisher would like to acknowledge the financial assistance of
the Canada Council for the Arts and the Ontario Arts Council, which is an
agency of the Government of Ontario.

 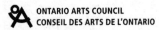

Published in Canada in 2009 by Exile Editions Ltd.
144483 Southgate Road 14
General Delivery
Holstein, Ontario, N0G 2A0
info@exileeditions.com
www.ExileEditions.com

Canadian Sales Distribution: U.S. Sales Distribution:
McArthur & Company   Independent Publishers Group
c/o Harper Collins   814 North Franklin Street
1995 Markham Road   Chicago, IL 60610
Toronto, ON M1B 5M8   www.ipgbook.com
toll free: 1 800 387 0117   toll free: 1 800 888 4741

For Martin Sherman, The Wise One:
As I casually mentioned in the Westbourne Grove veggie resto,
You are my cultural hero.

I press my face into the crisp white cotton of his shirts,
brush my cheek against his jackets,
sweaters still warm with him...
I remember the days of savage adoration,
child for father, father for child...

From *Soja, by* Rishma Dunlop

FIGHT AND FLIGHT

London, England – April 2002

People always say "It happened so fast." Actually, when you see it happen, it happens faster than that. The going is barely seen at all – an air-jostling movement, a flash of colours. What fills the room, what sustains, what I will see always, is the gone. The gone, with sky and clouds behind it.

Petra grabbed my childhood red leather chair, hurled it through the open window, and flew out after it. She thought she was half bird. A Storm Petrel. What bird watchers call "an accidental." I save animals. It's what I do. I've saved birds. I could not save Petra. She flew out and down, straight down, nine storeys.

Staring at the gone, I believed Petra's flight was my fault. I had just told her, a woman who thought she was a bird, I had told this bird-woman that our father – whose love she wanted enough to kill him for denying it to her – that he could fly. That I had seen him do this, had seen him fly. She spread her arms and tried to join him, to be with him where the rest of us could not follow. Not without first dying.

The gone filled with people. Dan stood in front of me, reached for me. I backed away. He kept saying Liss, Liss, Liss. Davy's hand rested lightly on my shoulder. I heard people running up the stairs. They overwhelmed the room, saying all these names, all names for me. So many hissy esses. Liss, Lissa, Ellissa. The guard from downstairs said Missus Major. There were other words, transformed inside my head to Petra's speedy buzzing, amplified. A thousand bees. The loudest buzz, the loudest name, came from someone who was not in the room.

I'd heard the name since the day I was born.

Ellissina.

BEFORE:
VANISHMENT, VIGILANCE, FREEDOM

County Galway, Ireland – 1962

Normally, if that word can be used in my family, I did not accompany my father to his divorce settlements. He brought me to the west of Ireland because I wanted to see Helena, the wife he was divorcing. I was ten.

The three of us lunched at O'Donovan's Seaside Café, our old favourite. Helena asked what I was doing at school, at home and anywhere else she could think of. I answered with as much information as it took to fill a hole. After, we hugged, promising to stay in touch. She drove off in a pale green van. I pretended to be fine.

Papp then drove us to what he called "the divorce place."

As instructed, I waited in our rented car as his black cashmere-coated back disappeared into the two-storey white building with its slanted low-hanging black tar roof and black-lettered white wooden sign swinging in the chill damp air – "Halloran and Halloran. Barristers and Solicitors."

My eyes never left the door through which my father had disappeared. I'd read and heard about vanishing parents, vanishing children. Preventing vanishment required vigilance. Despite my British accent and manner, I was the daughter of two Sicilians and understood vigilance.

I also knew well the weird wildness of children's books. Based on these books, and to keep from worrying too much about not being able to see exactly where Pappino was, I made a list in my head:

Fairy-tale dangers requiring vigilance.

People-eating wolves dressed up as your grandmother.

Armies of dwarves failing to shelter girls from poisoned apples.

Princesses held prisoner in towers.

Children who vanish into witchy houses made of gingerbread and rainbow-coloured sweets.

The list wasn't enough to keep me properly vigilant. It needed to mention my father. I added "Fathers vanishing into buildings." And then went on to magic words. Magic words were reputed by my family to be helpful with vigilances – especially the Italian ones. Saying them aloud warded off *malocchio* – the evil eye. I softly repeated the name of Pappino's hat – *Bor-sa-li-no.*

I believe that children, even if they are not Sicilian, see danger almost all the time. Adults are too busy being adults to see or remember the dangers they once saw, once knew. Children are in danger because they are small; adults are in danger because they are not children.

Vigilance, lists and magic words worked. Pappino re-emerged, alongside a short man with a fuzzy face (if this man were not human, I thought, he would be a terrier). Papp and Fuzzyface shook hands.

Our rented car was shiny, the colour of an aubergine. He opened the driver's side door and, quickly squeezing my woollen legging-ed knee, settled in, grinning his "I love to drive" grin. I felt hollowed out about losing Helena as a family member, but pleased to have successfully protected my protector. That protector was once again sitting beside me. I was, as he would say, "covered." I waited for the car version of the Choices Speech, silently counting. It came between 9 and 10.

"Ah. Driving. Driving gives you choices, Ellissina. If it's not good where you are, you get in the car and go somewhere else. Choices are freedom. Choices make you . . . more alive. Marriage is hard. Cuts down choices. Even when you love somebody, less choice makes it hard to breathe." He rolled down his window and the big car filled with Irish winter air.

"Breathe, Ellissina, breathe!"

We breathed and laughed and sang all the way to the airport.

We were cold but we were free, my father and I. We had choices. And we had each other.

MATTERS OF
LIFE AND DEATH

Southwold, Suffolk, England – January 2002

Three in the morning. The double-ring of the cordless phone wakes Dan and me. It being my bedroom and my phone, I reach across him and lift the receiver.

The caller is my mother. I receive information and replace the phone in its cradle.

"Wha?" Dan mumbles, shaking his head, forcing his eyes slightly more open than slits.

"My mother. With a message from my father."

"Your mother? I thought they'd not spoken for donkey's years."

"Forty. Forty years, two donkeys. Doesn't matter. What matters is that he's had congestive heart failure and is . . . trying, at eighty-nine, to not die. I have to go. Now."

"Of course. I'll drive you up to London."

I turn on both bed-lamps, moving quickly as I pack, sorting my passport and papers. "If you would, Dan, you can drive me to Heathrow. Papp is in Canada. In a Montréal hospital."

I ring the Hotel Vieux Quartier and book a room for "some time, tonight. I'll confirm the exact time from the airport."

I ring Betty at her home.

"Sorry to wake you, Bet. Can you be chief vet at the clinic for a bit? My father's been hospitalised in Canada. Cardio."

Betty immediately agrees, and assumes I'll be at my father's flat.

"No. A hotel. Easier to fully focus on the medical stuff that way . . . and I don't want to be at Papp's until he's there too."

CROWD CONTROL
Ste. Bernadette's Hospital – Montréal 2002

The small space between the nurses' station and the four even smaller rooms comprising the Intensive Cardiac Care Unit filled with all shapes, shades, ages and sexes of people – a compressed version of the human glut outside hotels when starry people and ersatz celebrities are inside. As usual in such situations, a sprinkling of camera-people seemed geometrically placed; legs apart, black cameras and large long zoom lenses thrusting forward.

Despite "Silence!" signs everywhere (the same word in both Canada's official languages), something had set off the crowd and an accretion of polyglot babble bounced off the walls. It reminded me of Southwold clinic when a nervous Pomeranian had an anxiety attack. Within minutes we'd have every dog barking, every cat meowing and Mrs. Mainwaring's American parrot, who always seemed to have an appointment at the same time as the neurasthenic Pom, repeatedly squawking "Get stuffed!" in a bird version of male basso. (Mrs. Mainwaring said this particular bit of parroting reminded her of "the late Mister Mainwaring, God rest him.")

Always afraid of crowds, indeed of anything that might turn violent, I hung back next to the *ascenseur*/elevator.

A woman I would come to know as Nurse Robitaille tried, in her second language, to whisper loudly in a modulated voice appropriate to Intensive Care Units: "Pee-pull! Pee-pull! You must all leave unless you are *intime* family. This area is for the very sick. It is very necessary that it be completely quiet. M'sieu' Major must not be deranged! You must all go to *premier* floor now and sign your name and relationship to the patient and perhaps more late in the week next it is possible that you can return."

They ignored Nurse Robitaille, but could not ignore the four large men who, toward the end of her entreaty, were herding them to the lifts and stairs. Some held children in front of themselves, insisting that these human shields were beloved of Johnny Major. Others swore they were close relatives. I did not recall seeing any of them before. Except Mignon Gravel, a stripper who'd dated my father for a week. I had seen her before and had no desire to see her again.

Holding my pass aloft, I managed to escape being sucked into the jostling, grumbling, exiting mass.

Finally, except for the clicks, taps and whirr of machines, there was quiet.

In the silence and skin-yellowing fluorescence, I introduced myself.

"Ah, Doctor Major. You are here, on my list. You have come from England, yes?"

"Yes. May I go to my father?"

"Of course. I will take you."

TUBULAR

A clear plastic bag of porridgy beige goo rotated over and over, flopping like soft thick flesh being worked by a masseur. Black lettering on the side of the bag identified the goo as "Nutritional Supplement – 01-07-02."

A television screen to the right of this goo-bag showed only one program – my father's heartbeat – what he had called "the tiny pine trees" during his first brief heart-related hospitalisation, ten years earlier.

A sound accompanied the picture: tha-THUMP, tha-THUMP. Sometimes the sound would halt almost imperceptibly and then begin again: Tha-THUMP, tha-THUMP.

A thin black tube extended from the bag. It ended inside Pappino's stomach. Other tubes ended inside other parts of him – his mouth, his throat, the crook of his left arm, and, I think (but never sought to know), one inside his penis and another up into his anus.

He lay there, large and lion-headed in the narrow bed, chestnut-brown eyes closed, oxygen-prongs in his nose, feeding him additional air as the slightly irregular tiny pine trees moved across the telly screen. The John Major Heart Show. I sank, heavy with travel, into a green Naugahyde chair next to the bed, gripping its silvery metal arms.

"Hello, Pappino mio," I whispered. Then, a bit louder, "Hello, John Major." John Major – the same name as that slightly bewildered boyish man who'd succeeded Margaret Thatcher as British Prime Minister.

That other John Major had little to do with my life, even as Prime Minister. The John Major lying in the narrow bed floating between some sort of here and some sort of there – the one I knew as Pappino – had everything to do with my life.

Nurse Robitaille silently studied my father and his assorted monitors and attachments, moving him, moving things, wiping his face with a wet towel.

"Has he awakened at all?" I asked.

"He opened his eyes, very, very wide, two times. But this means nothing with coma. I do not believe he actually saw me, saw anything. But you probably know about the open eyes seeing nothing. You are a doctor, non?"

"I'm a vet – a small-animal veterinarian. Dogs, cats, some domestic rodents, reptiles and birds."

"Ah, I see. That must be . . . fun."

"It's a good job to have in England. The English aren't always certain how they feel about *people* but they know they love animals. By extension, some affection is given to those of us who help to keep those animals healthy . . . Has my mother been here? Missus Douglas Robertson? It was she who phoned me."

Nurse Robitaille consulted her clipboard.

"She is on my list but you are the first to arrive. Mister Major's sister Antoinetta telephones every day but you are the first to actually be here. I will leave you now with your father. You know where the call button is and you are just across from . . . ."

"The nurses' station. Yes. I know. Thank you."

Nurse Robitaille said *"Bienvenue"* and quietly closed the door, leaving me to wonder about Mammina. Why had she, who had not spoken to my father for so long, who avoided even speaking *about* him – how and why had she been the one to notify me about his illness?

BASTINA

My parents were *impossibili insieme* – impossible together. She was, he said, the great, crazy love of his life. He also told me that the fights they had were "fucking dangerous. This tiny woman, she would come at anyone, *anyone*, and not back off. Not ever. If your mother had been a large man, she would've been heavyweight champion of the world!"

They were careful not to fight in front of me, but I saw it once, when I was three. My father, who Auntie Nan always said was built like a football star, had his head lowered, crossed arms and big hands over his face.

"Ellissa, please. Please stop. I don't want to fight you . . . if I fight you, I'll hurt you. Please stop, please!"

Mammina kept swinging at him, slapping hard at his shoulders, his chest, spitting anger-larded whisper words, in English and Italian – "screwing around," "whores," "blondes," "*stronzate*," "disgrace."

Then they saw me standing in the doorway to their bedroom. Mammina stopped instantly. She laughed and said "It's all right, Ellissina. We are only playing."

Usually my mother did not say stupid unbelievable things. It was not all right. They were not playing. I knew this. They knew I knew. I looked at them the way I always looked at grownups when they thought I might be stupid. My father reached out a hand towards me. I ignored it, turned and went to my room. He followed.

I lay in bed, covers pulled up, ignoring my father, who sat at the bed's edge.

"Little Bastina," he said. "When it's too much, you just stop. That's a good thing, Bastina. You must just stop. Until everything gets less crazy."

He kissed the back of my head, then got up and walked towards my bedroom door.

"I love you, Bastina," he said from the doorway.

"I love you too, Pappino," I replied almost inaudibly.

"I heard that, Ellissina-Bastina. I heard that and I'm very glad."

After that, I would stay in my room when craziness erupted at the other end of the flat in the night, from the room in which my parents were supposed to be asleep.

I was almost four when they divorced. My father moved to London to be with Jennifer Applewhite, a newsreader for the BBC, who would ultimately become the second of his divorces. ("A sweet civilised woman. The mother of my son. An amicable settlement.")

He was having a great success with his Montréal "Cognoscenti" restaurant and club, and opened a second one in London's Sloane Square; this one in a three-storey house, with an entire floor devoted to a casino.

At five, I went to live with him in London. They let it be my decision. We all agreed that I could change my mind any time after one school year.

I loved both parents, but felt safer with my father. My mother had a lot of rage inside her. It would come suddenly and leave once she ranted it away. She never hit me, but, having seen the rage, I moved closer to the parent I felt would shelter me best. And who adored me.

I attended the Jennifer Wedding, just outside London in Maidenhead-on-Thames. A six-piece band called a palm-court orchestra played slow dreamy dance music. Pappino, movie star handsome in his tuxedo, waltzed me around a circular white-walled, many-windowed room, his hands firmly encircling my waist, my white-socked feet atop his shiny black shoes. At the end of our waltz, he picked me up and swung me around, saying, "You are my adorable Ellissina! And I adore you!" People applauded and laughed.

Though I'd not told him this, I didn't want my father to be married to anyone other than my mother. Jennifer, however, was a sweet woman – slim, gentle and soft-spoken. Four months after the marriage, I had a blond baby brother.

My first London school, which I loved, had been Beatrix Potter's childhood home. I called it "Peter Rabbit School."

July was with my mother in Sicily (Taormina, where she'd been born. Sun. Sea. Fresh tomatoes. Two chickens, a rooster and a brown-and-white floppy-eared goat in the yard. Fresh eggs and strange-tasting goat milk).

Twice a year, Mammina came to England to be with me – one trip including both Christmas and my January 1st birthday, and the other in late June, to collect me for Taormina. Even before she married Dr. Doug, she would not see my father, not even on her Christmas visits ("It's better this way. You are what we have that is good. The rest – a mistake").

MAREIKE

Mareike DeLyn Major, wife # 5, came straight for me.

Her lips had become a hybrid mutation of labial and labia. Wildly puffed up, they looked like plump soft Italian sausages that had been lip-shaped and painted a glossy bright red. Oh God, I thought, don't kiss me with those things – if you kiss me with those things, they could explode, covering my cheeks in sticky, pulpy red sausage guts.

She did not kiss me. True to her socioethnic-group, the Dutch Former Film Stars, she air-kissed – near, but in no contact with, each cheek.

I was then enfolded in a combination of silver-fox fur, *Acqua di Parma* (a scent usually worn by my father) and some sort of chemical fruit face peel (the owner of one of my dog-patients used the same stuff. Smelled like sour aged cider).

"Let me look at you," Mareike said, holding me away. Fair enough, I thought; you look, I look.

She had to be somewhere in her seventies, but her face and neck were unlined and drum-tight. The wig was a dark ash-blonde pageboy. "She looks like Hamlet in drag," Davy would later note. Her makeup was, as ever, perfect, if a bit much in fluorescent hospital lighting.

Apart from the red sausage-lips, her eyes were the most compelling feature. Bright blue and opened wide, wide, wide, as Pappino's coma-eyes must've been.

Papp's startled eyes probably meant he was trying to be, but was not, conscious. Mareike's startled eyes were a surgical over-correction. She was entirely conscious. In my experience, the only creature more conscious than Mareike was the hungry wolverine that had been brought to me in a leg-hold trap. He had gnawed off his back right paw trying to get free. We kept him at the clinic until he was healed and could hobble about quite quickly for what Betty called "a tripod." I felt slight guilt knowing I would not do this for Mareike – who was probably too cunning to get caught in a leg-hold trap anyway.

"I came as soon as I could, dear. I knew you would be here, that your father would not be alone. Bless you for being such a good daughter. My brood of Majors comes tomorrow. It took me a while to find them. To find Floris, at least. Petra is usually in her Amsterdam flat, making things. She tends not to answer her phone. I know she's there. Just listening. And can only hope she will ring me back. It's maddening, really."

She turned abruptly from me, shouting "Brandy!"

My Christ, I thought, she wants a drink?!

A tall, well-tailored man with sleek shoe-polish black hair and rather a lot of gold jewellery, appeared at her side.

"Brandy, this is Ellissa. A fellow-Italian, as I told you on the plane. Johnny's daughter by his very first marriage. Ellissa, I would like you to meet a dear friend, Count Fillippo Brandoni!"

"*Molto piacere, Signora*," said Mareike's Count, with a slight nod of his head and a flash of enormous hyperwhite dental work.

"Thank you, Count Brandoni, for accompanying my former step-mother all the way from Rome. I hope you had a pleasant flight."

I said this in my heaviest Sicilian dialect. I speak a reasonably good Romanesco (not upmarket Florentine, though borderline acceptable to the Italian nobility), but Pappino's tube-tied bedroom was next to where we were standing. I knew that if he could hear me speaking Sicilian to a pompous prat, it would make him proud and make him laugh.

The Count's reaction was as expected. His Chiclet-tooth smile froze in a rictus and his long strong nose twitched, twice, as if some-one had passed wind. He recovered quickly from having been grazed by Southern Italian, and said, in perfect English: "It is, I understand, a sad occasion; a potentially sad occasion, and I wished to be here for Mareike, should she have need of me."

Behind him, I saw that Jen had arrived. She stood a cautious distance behind Mareike, quiet and patient. "Please excuse me for a moment. Thank you. *Grazie.*"

I walked between Mareike and the Count, and took Jennifer's hands in my own. "Thank you for coming, Jen. Have you visited with Johnny?"

"Hello, Elissa. I was going to do that now."

"It's two at a time. Like Noah's Ark. I'll wait here, give you some time alone."

"Thank you. It will be our only visit – until he is well. I must be at the BBC by tomorrow evening. I'm sure Davy will stay for as long as you need him."

"Davy. Is Davy here?"

"He was not at the hotel, but I know he's due today. We spoke last night. He said he was on his way."

"That's good news. And Anna? Are you two still the Major Ex-Wives' Club? Is she coming?"

"She can't leave Sweden – it's the middle of exam grading at Stockholm University. She sent a note and flowers."

Mareike, having swiftly moved into hearing range, laughed lightly. "Anna? The number four wife? They were only married for a few months. I'm sure she's a lovely woman but . . ."

"Yes. I like Anna very much. As does my father. Someone's removed her flowers and note. Where . . . ?"

"They're there, Ellissa dear. I took the liberty of placing them in a corner of the window, where the sun could shine through the freesia. Just behind the balloons."

"Balloons?"

"Yes dear. Happy balloons. I got them at the hospital gift shop."

Three incredibly ugly silver-foil helium balloons, shaped like inflated pancakes, were tied to the Naugahyde chair. On each one was written the word "Congratulations!" Mareike never failed to exceed my most surreal expectations:

Congratulations, Johnny, on not waking up.

Congratulations on being helpless.

Congratulations on dying before I do.

Congratulations on having to eat through a tube and shit through a tube.

Congratulations on having a braying menagerie outside your room hoping to be remembered in your will.

Congratulations.

"Well, Ellissa dear, I do need to find my wayward girls. I told Floris, and asked her to tell Petra, if she can find Petra, to meet us at the Hotel Vogue. Fillippo and I will go there now to collect Floris. We will also have a bit of food, and then, naturally, return."

"Naturally."

Jennifer left, after asking me to please let her know if she could help in any way.

I entered Papp's room, tied the hideous balloons to a coat-hook and sat like a sack of rocks in the Naugahyde chair, exhausted as always, even without jet lag, by contact with Mareike.

"Hullo, you poor old Naugus," I whispered, patting the chair and remembering Davy's silly old routine, the one we would do as teenagers, when playing Major's Music Hall.

"It's Naugahyde. I shot the Naugus myself. On Safari. Safari it's the only Naugus I've shot."

And I would reply: "You *shot* the Naugus? Oh, Captain Wankworthy, the Naugus is an engendered species!"

"As are we all, dear lady, to the best of our ability. As are we all."

We all, I thought, are about to have a Major Family Crazy.

Mareike, Floris and Petra

Floris and Petra had been porcelain dolls as babies and into their mid-teens – an Aryan fairytale fantasy of mirror-image duplication. When they were born, Pappino, in that way men can be, was wildly impressed with his accomplishment.

"Two of 'em! I made two at once! And they're perfect. So pretty. Come, Ellissina, come to Amsterdam and see your new sisters!"

I got permission to leave school and flew to Amsterdam, missing the first two study days of How to Ameliorate Feline Glaucoma.

Mareike had been one of the Netherlands' best-known film actresses, but Dutch stardom doesn't always export. She had tried, doing films in France and Italy. Neither the French nor the Italians were interested, so she returned to being the biggest sexy cinema shark in the Dutch pond. Until she met my father and graduated to "former Dutch film star" – which required no film work and yielded considerably more money.

Mareike, in her role of new mother, sat propped up in bed, a baby at each of her always-large breasts; long wavy blonde hair tied back in a low ponytail. I wondered if it were a wig. She had, even then, a formidable collection of well-made wigs. Usually, I could only tell when she'd go from long and cascading to short bob and then back in a three-day period.

She wore a cream satin nightie with matching unbuttoned peignoir and was fully made up for filming. "Helloooo, Ellissa dear. How lovely of you to come and share in our blessed event. You look wonderful! Such clear skin you have, no need for cosmetics. You're lucky. Olive skin. Darker. Italian actresses have skin like yours. Me, I look a fright. I had such a long and difficult labour. And my hair looks dreadful. Needs a wash. So, voila! Ponytail. Not my best look, but it keeps hair out of the babies' eyes."

Thirty-two years ago, she was already forty-something (no one, including Pappino, knew her precise age) and taking all sorts of fertility hormones. Even Papp, who did want to make more babies, complained that he "didn't marry the woman to take her temperature three times a day."

The induced delivery had been what Davy called Mareike's Last Bitch Effort. Heiresses. Which, of course, was the point. My father, in testosterone frenzy about his double-header, did not see the point about heiresses.

Eventually the point became impossible to miss. Mareike and daughter Floris got into scrapes of every bimbo description (one of them involving a tango-dancing Brazilian proctologist named Cucu Laredo). They ran up huge bills all over Europe and parts of the United States. Lawyers, plastic surgeons, lovers and Paris/Milan couture proliferated, all charged to the credit cards of Mr. John Major. Finally, overwhelmed, offended, and ultimately infuriated, he turned off the taps.

Petra wasn't part of the Cash Cow Conspiracy, even when Floris bullied her, as she regularly did almost from birth. Petra's response to the compulsive avarice of her mother and sibling was to become anorexic and keep to herself, making mobiles out of beads, glass, bird feathers and wire. She was, however, twinned in Pappino's mind. As he had embraced two girls, he rejected two girls – a package deal gone bad.

Years later, when I'd go up to London to stay with him, he would sometimes speak in a sad, slightly angry, but not entirely unamused tone, about how "those three thought they could rip me off forever.

I'll support them for as long as I live. They carry my name, and none of 'em knows how to work. But I'm no golden goose and there aren't gonna be any eggs. Not for that gang. They think I don't see, don't know. How could I not know?"

Papp rubbed his large hands over his face in the way he did when trying to remember or forget something.

"Not that there aren't reasons for Mareike being this way. She grew up inside the Second World War, a teenage girl selling herself to whomever, whenever, for whatever. What she learned from this humiliation is that it's important to get a good price. You get one good price, then you don't have to sell yourself so many times. I was a good one. A very good price. Fine. I do business. I could do business with Mareike. I could stop loving her and just do business – could even enjoy it. She is, she can be . . . an exciting woman.

"But they shamed me in public. That was not part of any deal we had made, not part of any deal I would ever make with anyone. Mareike is in the tabloids all the time, with these oily gigolos. So is Floris. I loved those twins. I loved their mother. But they worked me and worked me and worked me until I couldn't take it any more. So, no golden eggs. The eggs belong to you. To you and your brother . . . your brother . . ."

"Davy."

"Right. John David. You know how I am with names."

"What's my name?"

He laughed, reached for my hand, squeezed it. "Your name? Elsie? No, not Elsie. Ellissa. Ellissina. Your name I can never forget. Even when I'm an old, old man. You're the best. You're all there is. The only one I really love. And whatsisname . . ."

"Davy."

"I knew that. You just told me. You and Davy are the two I can trust. And, you . . . you can cook."

I smiled. "You're telling me you're hungry, yes?"

"Yeah. Could you make us some pasta and salad? I don't want to go to Cognoscenti tonight. Just want to relax with you. Deal?"

"Deal . . . If you'll tell me how Lucky Luciano won the Second World War."

"Deal."

DAVY

"Even with a feeding tube for a cigar, he's got those great lips. The same ones as the Divine Antinous, lover of . . ."

"The Roman emperor Hadrian. Whew. I fell asleep. Hello, Davy. How long have you been here?"

"Only a few moments. More to the point, Lissa, how long have *you* been here?"

"Dunno exactly. I can tell you this chair is less than brilliant. Feels like hardened porridge to my fifty-year-old arse."

"Fifty-one, actually. The first twelve months don't have a year designation."

"Thanks ever so much for pointing out the extra bit of advancing decrepitude, *mon frère.*"

"You look knackered."

"I *am* knackered. We can't all be the direct descendoes of Dorian Gray. Good thing I'm sitting, as walking would be damn near impossible without my Zimmer frame. Listen, Davy Dazzler, if I can manage to hobble to you, might I have a hug?"

Davy opened his arms. Within seconds, I was nested inside his hug. He smelled of wool, aftershave, and his personal Davyness. I rested my head on his chest and wanted to weep, but didn't. I'd no idea how much Pappino was with us. If he could hear me crying, could connect to it, connect it to me, crying would worry him.

Breaking gently from the hug, I placed my hand against Davy's cheek, needing to keep our skin-contact.

"Re your 'sitting' inquiry, I have been mostly seated since my mother rang me in Southwold. Yesterday? I think that's right. Sat on the plane for about eight hours; then sat in a taxi. Now I sit here, in this creepy little room with the comatose eighty-nine-year-old version of the Divine Antinous . . . waiting, hoping, willing him to come back to us."

"Your *mother* rang you? I thought they never spoke."

"They never do. Before he decided to lay low in Comaville he told Auntie Nan that he wanted my mother to notify me . . ."

"It was Auntie Nan who rang *me*. Has she been here?"

"No. She checks in a few times a day by phone. What with Uncle Joe having been in hospital for so long, and so recently dying, Auntie Nan, to use her exact words 'Can't take hospitals.' She asked me to contact her immediately if things get better or worse. She and Uncle Joe married as teenagers. This is all hard for her."

"What about your mum? Will she be here?"

"She says no. Auntie Nan agrees, says there's no point in having her fly all the way from Vancouver until we know more. If there is a better or worse, Auntie Nan will call her immediately. So, for the moment, it's me."

"And now me too, Lissa."

Davy looked out at the heavy snowfall on the Rue St. Denis.

"Crikey! It's still comin' down! We landed in this mess. Thought the plane was going to figure skate into the sea."

"River. And welcome to Montréal. This is standard winter weather here. I fetched my Canadian snow-gear from Pappino's local flat. There's lots of warm and woolly men's clobber there if you need anything."

"Papp's clothes would be hoodge on me." He held out puffy bright yellow arms. "I'm good. This jacket is a bomber-style box-stitched duvet. Tariq's. He's also given me ankle-to-neck thermal undies and Highland woollen trousers, Campbell tartan. Not to mention a super-heavy designer polo-neck from when he did the sets and costumes for that Finnish opera."

"Did Tariq come with you?"

"Couldn't. Nothing to wear. Joke. Actually, he's designing this enormo ugly musical; I mean they *want* ugly! The airhead who owns the theatre also owns a department store. So the set will look like Taste of the World – International Fine Furnishings. Besides, he did one recent New York trip and felt targeted for having an Arab name, even though he was born in London. Says they treated him like a terrorist."

"Tariq a terrorist? Funny picture."

"Yeh. 'I am going to stab and shoot and kill you, Madam, but first let me do something about these curtains. Vomit-green on an aeroplane! What were they thinking?'"

We laughed. I realised I'd not done that since arriving at the hospital. "It's good to laugh."

"I can probably get you to do it at least once more if you'll let me buy you a proper French coffee. Can you leave your post?"

"Oh sure. This is a hospital. I'm just afraid . . . if anything changes . . ."

"How is he?"

"They say he's 'stable.' There's a good place next door. We'll tell the desk person. I'd love a coffee. Hell, I *need* a coffee."

"Let's do it, *sorella mia*."

"*Sorella mia*? Not bad Italian for a half Brit. Bravo."

"*Grazzi*."

"*GRAT*see. *Tsee*, Not 'zee.' *Andiamo*. Let's go. That's '*in-din-di-EEMU*' in proper Sicilian."

"Proper Sicilian? Isn't that a contradiction."

"Go."

"With a Sicilian behind me. You think I'm crazy?"

"Only half. Go!"

DAVY AND LISSA'S
MAJOR MUSIC HALL SHOW

"It's good to have you here, in the middle of this zoo. To be part of Lissa and Davy's Major Music Hall Show."

"Davy and Lissa's Major Music Hall Show."

"Fine. Have top billing. You're the professional."

"Ta. Top and bottom can be important. A propos, you still dating the Southwold Plod?"

"Dan Rhodes is not the 'Southwold Plod,' Davy. He's the Detective Chief Inspector of the Southwold Constabulary – the top cop."

"Begging pardon, madam. Are you still having an enshagment with the top cop then?"

"Yes. Almost four months now."

"Does it matter?"

"More to him than me. He knows this I think. We sort of talk around it. He intimates. I evade. Then we have dinner. But . . . we're good. He's a kind and decent man. We celebrated my birthday the night before I got Pappino's news. He bought me a beautiful peignoir. It's all a bit . . . gauzy, but I will wear it for him. Funny. We're at our best naked."

"That happens."

"I know."

"Me too. Which reminds me – 'birthday' reminds me, not 'naked' – I brought you a birthday gift."

Davy handed me a small rubber nun. "Squeeze it," he said. I did. It barked. The people at the next table looked at us, whispering in French. I pretended not to notice. "Uh . . . thanks."

"People always gave you goofy barking dogs. I was fairly certain that you didn't have a goofy barking nun."

"I did not have a barking nun."

"You do now."

"Yes, I do now. And not a moment too soon."

At that moment, inside our shared scary, Davy's presence, goofy gift and all, was the second best thing that could happen to me. He has what I call "a dear face." Big brown eyes (our father's eyes), with the longest pale lashes and his mother's curly blond hair and slightly upturned nose. His wide smile is perfect for children's theatre, in which he frequently works. On that snow-mad father-vigil day I sat across from him at Café au Coin loving that face and grateful to see it.

"Crikey, Lissa, it's lovely to have a hot bev. Stunningly bloody cold in this country!"

I laughed.

"I told you I'd have you laughing again. But I'm not certain I know why."

"It's 'Crikey' – we're part of an ever-diminishing group of Brits under the age of seventy who say 'Crikey' all the time. Did you get it from Papp?"

"Yeh. And from the BBC."

"Papp got it from me. And I got it from the Lord's Name Rule at Peter Rabbit School. It was considered sacrilegious to say 'Christ' or 'God' – not to mention deeply non-u and vulgar. 'Crikey' and 'Gosh' were the school-endorsed substitute words. Papp didn't know any of that. He just liked it because it made him feel like an English toff – the same way Cognoscenti made him feel like an Italian toff."

"And because he says it, we say it."

"Yeh."

"When I was a boy the word made me feel closer to Papp. You two didn't need that. You were already close."

"I know he loves you, Davy. It's just harder for men to . . ."

I warmed my hands on the white bowl of café au lait. "When we were kids, after the divorce . . . did Pappino see you enough?"

"Pappino. I never did call him that. Brits don't have Pappinos."

"*Pappini*. The plural is '*Pappini*.'"

"See what I mean? You know the plural – I barely manage the singular. Besides, I looked it up – Pappino means 'little father.' There is nothing little about our father."

I shook my head, smiling. "Pappino started because my mother was Mammina. She's tiny, but more than makes up for it in power."

"Yeah well, 'Pappino' was more Italian than felt right coming out of my little Brit face, in my little Brit voice. The most I could manage was 'Papp.' As to 'seeing me enough,' I dunno. Once we weren't under the same roof, it was not as much, but rather a lot until I went away to school. He did visit school. Came to see my 'Romeo.' I think he was relieved that his son wasn't the boy playing Juliet. I told him that, in Shakespeare's time, men played all the parts – even when it wasn't at a boys' school. He nodded and said he'd heard that, but I know he was happier not being Juliet's father. Later, when it became clear that I was gay, he pulled away for a while – we've never spoken about it. Papp belongs to a generation of straight men that'd rather not think about gay men. But he always said . . . says that I'm 'a good kid.' A good forty-five-year-old kid, that's me. For a divorced father, he was, and still is, a . . . solid, loving presence in my life. Not like the two of you though. You were like a two-headed single being. Some of it is father-daughter. Fathers are, I think, besotted with their girl children. But it wasn't just that. You were the big and little of this . . . this glorious Mediterranean thing. And speaking of Wops, let us raise an espresso cup to the poor horse who gave his life so Marunkle's Count – the 'o' is silent – could have teeth!"

"That's funny, Davy, and don't say Wop to a Wop."

"You say it all the time."

"That's different. I am a Wop."

"I'm half a Wop."

"Right. So you can say it half as often as I do . . . and you've used up your quota for tonight. So, no more 'Wop' or the Ministry for Ethnically Stereotypical Activities will send two guys named Guido to your house. They will break both your legs."

"Oh no! Not that! The short actorines in children's theatre have to play dogs, cats and kiddies . . . in that order."

"What do you imagine the Count and Mareike play at? In bed? Cuddles?"

"Oh Lissa, cuddling would be the best that pair could manage. The Countess is Martha, not Arthur. My team, not yours."

"You sure?"

"Dead cert . . . which does not mean that old Marunkle, who is something of a fellatial legend, doesn't occasionally . . . go down for the Count."

This observation produced more laughter.

"You've the best laugh in the family. Papp loves your laugh. Says it's like your mother's when they first met."

"Well, Little Bruvver, do you know where I got my laughter? From you. When you came into my life, you brought funny with you. And your funny gave me laughter. Neither our father nor my mother is terribly funny, except inadvertently."

"True. Papp doesn't do jokes. And no matter what Papp says, I cannot imagine your mum laughing. She scares me witless."

"She does have a soft side."

"I'll take your word for it. And I'm delighted that you've inherited your belated sense of humour from me."

"Me too, she said gravely. No, not 'gravely.' 'Seriously.' Let's not have any words with 'grave' in them."

"Yeah. 'Grave's' pretty deadly."

"Shut up."

"Me too. Must be the salt water."

"What?"

"Nothing. Old music hall joke. Learned them all at me master's knee, in Repertory TheaTAH."

"Which master's knee?"

"Various masters. Various knees."

How Pappino
Protected His Chest

We walked back to the hospital, heads lowered against the snowfall. In the Intensive Cardiac Care room, Pappino was as we'd left him: face calm, eyes closed, goo-bag rotating, white pine trees moving across the black screen.

"How does this work, Lissa? Is it like the National Health in the UK? How does Papp meet the residency requirements for Montréal when he lives in London?"

"Through classic Papp moves. He owns the building that Auntie Nan manages. Keeps an apartment there. Maintains his Canadian passport and carries enough travellers' insurance to protect a village . . . oh, he also has regular checkups with Doctor Belliveau, built the children's wing of this hospital and bought them a lot of expensive equipment. It isn't just Pappino protecting his chest. This city started him. He loves the place and visits whenever he can. He was a beneficiary and now can be a benefactor."

"Both. A 'factor' and a 'ficiary.'"

"Exactly."

I sank into the Green Naugus, rubbing my face.

"Look Lissa, you've been on duty for a while. Why don't you have a proper sleep at the hotel?"

"It's . . . about vigilance. The Nether, Nether Land sisters are coming."

"Florid and Petrified?"

Our old secret names for Floris and Petra. "Yes, Florid and Petrified."

"I can handle them. I'll stay with him. Have a sleep, Lissa. You need strength."

"Yeh. I will need strength for . . . the *pazzeria*, the madness to come."

I hugged him, then wrapped my black, down-filled hooded coat around me and pulled on red wool gloves. Davy kissed me in the centre of my forehead – something Pappino always did. (Did Davy know this? Did Papp do it with him as well? Was it an inherited trait?) He sat in the Naugahyde chair, looked at Pappino, blew out a long whooshing breath.

"Davy?"

He turned.

"He told me, often, that he loves you. That you and I are his 'real kids,' the 'ones who earn their own damn money' . . . the only ones he trusts. For about twelve years though, I think the twins were his favourites. He never said it, but, for a while, I think he loved the twins best."

"Until he loved them least."

"Exactly."

BABY BOXER

If I'd had any childhood doubts about Pappino's power, they were dispelled when I was seven, in my second year at Peter Rabbit School.

Mrs. Tipton, Head of Beatrix Potter Day School, was married to an ex-footballer turned sports journalist. They had a son. Berwick. He called himself Berry. Our first meeting was at a school social. We wore nametags. Berry's, pinned to his jacket, read "Berwick Tipton." We were meant to introduce ourselves to at least three strangers. So I said "Hullo, Berwick Tipton. I'm Ellissa Major."

Berry hated being called Berwick. He waited for me after school and told me this while he beat me up. Blood, bruises and a split lip.

The Tiptons were having dinner when my father arrived, unannounced, at their home, wounded girl-child in tow. Standing in the arched entry to the Tipton dining room, he said, "Good evening. I'm John Major. Your boy, Berwick Tipton, who does not wish to be called Berwick, did this to my daughter, Ellissa Major. Ellissa is very happy at your school, and is excelling there. Therefore, I am pleased to contribute annually to this school."

Pappino paused for a moment, running his right hand through his hair, then continued. "If your son ever touches my daughter again, or harms her in any way, I shall select a boy of his size and weight – to be fair, you understand – and will stand in attendance – also to be fair – while this boy I've selected beats the crap out of your boy, a boy, your boy, who hits girls. After that, I will, as a non-violent rational adult, sue you personally, as well as your school, for a considerable sum of money. Are we clear?"

Mrs. Tipton had been saying "mm, mm" and nodding her head in agreement for a while. Mr. Tipton finally spoke. "You have been perfectly clear, Mister Major . . . and entirely justified. We will . . . deal appropriately with Berwick." Papp smiled, lips closed, nodded, thanked the Tiptons for their understanding and, still holding my hand, turned to leave. At the door, he faced them again, saying, "And for God's sake, change the boy's name. Ellissa didn't know he hates being called Berwick . . . but crikey, wouldn't you?"

My non-violent rational adult father then took me home and taught me to box. ("Keep your hand up, protect your face, keep moving, don't pull the punch! Follow through! Hit straight out, hard! Now hook, hook, and come up from under. You're pulling, don't pull back! Follow through! Always use your non-punching hand to protect your face. Four protection zones: Jaw. Mouth. Nose. Eyes. Again. Jaw! Mouth! Nose! Eyes! Now, change hands. I *know* it's your weak hand. If you're gonna box, you can't have a weak hand. Jaw! Mouth! Nose! Eyes! Punch! Straight out! Protect your chest! Always protect your chest! If there're more than one attacker, you go for the biggest one first. Keep moving. If it's impossible, if you're really over-matched, and there's a large object you can lift, hit the nearest person with it, and keep swinging it until they run away.")

By midnight, I was a fairly decent seven-year-old female boxer. It was also true, then as now, that those who hit girls or women do not usually plan to box, and will likely deck their female opponent before she gets her fists up and assumes the stance. The part about hitting the adversary with a large object was comforting, though – quite helpful to think about when trying to appear brave.

HELENA

The hotel concierge handed me a fax. It was from Helena, my father's third wife. She and Davy had been the only people I called after Mammina notified me, leaving a message on her Ansaphone. In my room, I opened the fax. Helena was one of the rare people who could write as she spoke. It was good to hear her.

Dearest Ellissa

I'm so sorry to hear that John is unwell. Thank you for including me among those invited to visit with him.

I have thought a lot about this invitation. My time with John was extraordinary. I've never known anyone like him . . . and likely never shall. All that energy and surety. Fierce and fearless, he was.

He couldn't imagine a West Country Irish girl who did not ride. As you know, my mother suffered with all sorts of cancers during my school years. When not in class, I was with Ma, doing my schoolwork at her bedside, missing Gymkhana and other outdoor activities. I started weaving because it is something you can do at your mother's bedside.

John adores horses and rides wonderfully (which is remarkable, given that he did not learn until he was in his forties). When he fell in love, or something like love, with a ginger-haired weaver from the west of Ireland, her not riding was simply unacceptable. So he taught me to ride. I kept falling off the horse and he'd make me get back on. This continued for weeks. At one point he said "Christ! Look at you! If you don't learn to ride soon, you're gonna be too much of a mess to marry!"

I did learn to ride and we did marry.

Some of the best times were when we three rode together along the shore in Galway and then had smoked salmon sandwiches at O'Donovan's.

John and I shared sweet tenderness and strong attraction but neither of us had any idea who the other was. I grew up hoping a strong, handsome man would whisk me away from my small-town seafront life. I think I expected something like a modern Pirate King. Which, in many ways, was exactly what I got. He wanted to marry a Celtic myth. An Irish weaver with ginger hair fit the bill. On the bare bones of my looks and occupation, he superimposed what he needed to see and believe.

He would sit in his ornate, enormous Belgravia flat and watch me weave. I will weave wherever I am, but I did feel a bit ridiculous doing it in that flat.

Do you remember the 'Weavening Evenings?' Film stars, business people and mysterious Italian-American gentlemen retiring to the parlour after dinner and John asking me to weave for them? A silent harp recital. Helena, John's Irish Angel, plucking at her tuneless loom.

Then came The Weaver's House. I'd grown up in that small grey-stone Galway house. When it came up for sale, John bought it for me. He tried to spend time there – usually when you were with your mother or on a school trip – but he simply hated it. Said he hadn't worked all his life just to live in a draughty old house with cramped rooms and a ceiling that hit him in the head. He also complained of what he called "night mice" – said he could hear them scratching from inside the walls. John doesn't live in a house; he guards it, like a big black dog listening for danger. Or mice.

One morning, after a particularly noisy mouse-night, he declared that he could no longer abide the house, but that I was welcome to stay there whenever I wished. He returned to Belgravia, saying he would see me there, and looked forward to my return. I procrastinated and, after a few weeks, wrote him. I said – and meant it – he was wonderful and beautiful and brave . . . but that I wanted to live in my little house in Galway.

Obviously, it was about more than living quarters – we were simply two very different creatures. Time together amplified these differences.

When we divorced, I wanted only that house. John thought I'd be asking for money. "They all do," he said. He was genuinely surprised when my solicitor told him 'Mrs. Major only wants The Weaver's House.'

Mr. Halloran, my solicitor, told me your father said "Only that broken-down house? Are you sure? She's a weaver, for Chrissakes. What'll she live on?"

I live well (and, thanks to John, rent-free) – weaving, and teaching others to weave.

I am glad your handsome, buckle-swashing Italian father came, however briefly, into my life. I send him my prayers, from a draughty old mouse-house in Galway.

XO,
Helena

P.S. If you've time and inclination, do come visit me here. My husband, Dr. Jim Finnerty is, as you are, a veterinarian. He treats large animals, such as horses. We've two of our own – sweet beasts, both, and try to ride together every Sunday. When I last saw you, you were a lively child – a softer miniature of your father. It would be splendid to see who you grew up to be.

Of all my father's wives (including my combative mother), I'd most hoped Helena would be a keeper. She brought forth a loving gentleness in him. And the seaside horseback rides were a joy. They both looked so smashing in their riding clothes – my broad-shouldered black-haired father in his navy twill jacket, jodhpur trousers and shiny black boots and this lithe beautiful woman in a Galway brown tweed jacket, jeans and brown boots, with the sun shining through her curly Irish-Setter-coloured hair. I would deliberately ride a bit behind, just to watch them, to be one happy third of a sweet and loving family.

THE WICKED WITCH
OF THE NETHER LANDS

"Only you here, Davy? Any sign of Mareike and Floris? Petra?"

"Mareike has been here. There was . . . a bit of a scene. Doctor Belliveau is in his office. He wants to see you."

"Is Papp worse?"

"No. A bit better, actually. Opened his eyes for a moment, and seemed to smile at me. Then he sighed and closed his eyes again. There was . . . a different feeling to this eye-opening, so I rang for the doctor. Which was when . . . look, it would be good if you spoke to Belliveau, Lissa. He'll do better at explaining things. I'll wait for you here."

I wanted to stay in the room, to talk to Pappino, to see if he opened his eyes again, but Davy's tone was uncharacteristically urgent. I said I'd be right back and went quickly down the hall.

Dr. Belliveau asked me to sit. "Ellissa. Have you spoken with your brother?"

"Yes. A moment ago. He said there'd been some improvement in my father's condition, and that you wanted to see me."

He then told me that after Pappino and Davy's moment of recognition, he'd invited Davy to his office to discuss "possible protocols, both in the event of further improvement or if there is deterioration."

After their discussion, Davy went to get a coffee and the doctor returned to the Intensive Cardiac Care room. He found Mareike there, alone. Both her hands were filled with Pappino's support-tubes.

"The tubes were still properly connected to your father, but, given the intensity of her grip and concentration, it seemed to me that she intended to pull them out. I asked, loudly, what she was doing. She smiled and said she was moving the tubes away from your father's chest, to make him more comfortable. This was highly unlikely, most of the tubes not being *on* his chest, but, as they were all still connected, I could prove nothing – and didn't want to disturb Johnny's healing with . . . discord and accusations. It was more than a bit alarming. I told her to please let go of the tubes immediately. 'Of course, Doctor, I was only trying to help,' she said, still smiling.

"She then announced that, as 'John Major's legal wife,' she wished to sign a 'do not resuscitate' form. I explained that such a form is only valid when co-signed by his physician – that would be me – and also that his children and sister had a right to contest such a request."

I felt vertiginous nausea. And rage. "'John Major's legal wife?' They were divorced over twenty years ago."

"She said there was never a divorce . . . 'Not even a legal separation.' None of which alters the fact that she cannot sign a D.N.R. without my co-signing. And she certainly cannot unilaterally, surreptitiously, and manually cut off his life supports, even if she's his legal *mother*!"

"Is he really getting better? Can he still . . . clear this?"

"Ellissa, it's fifty-fifty. Perhaps forty-sixty. But, for a man his age, he has a strong constitution. And a fierce will to live."

"I just received a fax from Ireland that called him fierce. I think, to keep from screaming, I will concentrate on fierce." I stood up.

"Thank you, Doctor, for telling me this. And for . . . getting to my father in time. We will not leave him alone again."

"That's wise. If she is his legal spouse, I cannot bar her, but we do have a 'no-more-than two people' rule for the room. I've put all Intensive Care desk-staff on notice. They'll monitor Johnny more closely when she's here."

"Could extra monitoring also apply as well to her twin daughters, Floris and Petra?"

"I've not seen twin daughters. Have they been here?"

"Dunno. They're expected."

FLORIS

Floris's ass, as it had become since last I'd seen it, made me think of a round rock island. One of those places in the middle of a lake. Big enough to support one house and a rowboat with an outboard motor. You'd get from the mainland to Floris's ass using this boat.

The ass-island was bending over my father's bed. It was in blue denim jeans. I greeted it. She stood and faced me. Her ass went to the place that allows it to be called the behind.

The doll-like face had amazingly (or surgically) not bloated. It was a bit rounder. Round face, round, bright blue eyes, silent-movie lips, and the same cute little nose as her mother. Given to her by the same surgeon in Brazil. Her butter-blonde hair fell to just above her shoulders, in waves and ringlets around her face.

Years earlier, the twins attended English boarding schools and would sometimes stay at the London flat. Papp felt the girls would be safer with "an adult in the room." He installed pricey twin beds in my large bedroom. Though I said nothing at the time, *their* safety was not the problem. They'd close their eyes, pretending to be asleep. I'd lie awake looking at their golden hair. I thought it was the most beautiful hair in the world. I also knew that if I fell asleep while they were awake, they would hit me. Quick hard hits. When it happened, I'd open my eyes and they'd have theirs closed, feigning sleep. So I would stay awake, waiting to be sure they were truly asleep, looking at their hair.

"Hello, Ellissa. Mama said you were here. I knew you would be. Would be here. You look exactly the same. Papa doesn't look the same. Papa looks terrible! Is it awful for me to say that? I'm sorry. I shouldn't have said that. I'm sorry I said that."

She laughed the melodic irrelevant laugh that always accompanied this circular babbling, along with repeated tapping at the upper lip of her closed mouth with three fingers. Since childhood, she'd done this when she felt anxious. Sometimes she would also say "Bad Floris." Watching her do this as an overweight thirty-three-year-old, even without "Bad Floris," I wondered if she'd ever been slapped in the mouth. If so, by whom? Mareike? Some boyfriend of Mareike's? Surely not by my father.

"It's all right, Floris. He's quite ill. He does not look well. He is doing better though. Or so the doctor tells me. Is your mother here?"

"In the Little Girls' Room. She had lipstick on her teeth."

Never one to miss a cue, Mareike appeared in the doorway, all in dusty-pink and back in the Hamlet pageboy hair. My fists clenched involuntarily. A large object. Hit her with a large object. Hit her and hit her and hit her until she is a puddle of pulp and wig and fabric.

"Helloooo, everyone. I suppose you've heard the good news, Ellissa. Your father is improving. Only slightly mind you, but . . ."

"Yes, Mareike, I've been informed of . . . everything." She jerked her head back quickly, laughing lightly.

"Well, we now have a trio in the room, a quartet, including me. And I know that only two are permitted, so . . ."

"If you're gonna go, Mama, can I come with you? I'm hungry."

"Certainly, dear. Let's get a bit of . . . whatever meal this is the hour for."

Floris stood in front of me, very close. Too close. "Ellissa, I . . . you . . . look great . . . maybe we could . . . It's good to . . ."

"Come along, Floris. You'll have lots of time to visit with Ellissa. Come."

And trailing a melange of scents and odours, they left. I sank into the Naugahyde chair, wrapping my right hand around my fisted left wrist, biting down on my knuckles.

THE STICKS AND STONES MYTH

Years later, I told Pappino about the nocturnal childhood experiences.

"Why didn't you tell me the twins were hitting you?"

"I was an adult! My 'attackers' were two little girls with tiny hands. It wasn't Berwick Tipton at Peter Rabbit School."

"Who?"

"Berwick. When I was seven. At Beatrix Potter Day School. He beat me up, and you went to his parents – his mum ran the school – and . . ."

"Oh, yeah. I remember that. He hated his name. Had a faggy name."

"Papp, I do wish you wouldn't use that term."

"I'm sorry, Ellissina. I don't mean anything by it. It's a habit. Used it all my life. I don't say it around your brother."

"Yes, you do, actually. Not a lot, but you do. You don't hear it, but he does. It is, as you say, a habit."

"I've said that word in front of him?"

"You've said it when he could hear you. Once, on the phone with Sal, he heard you say 'In a way, I don't have any sons. My boy's a good kid, but he's a fag. So I guess I have four daughters.'"

"And he heard me say it?"

"Yes. He was sixteen and in the next room."

"That's awful, Ellissa. That's lousy."

"Not one of your better moments. Davy knows you love him, and he loves you. 'Fag' is just . . . not a great word."

"I'll be more careful. I don't want to hurt your brother. But you should've told me about those other little shits hitting you."

I didn't say that I'd been afraid. Not afraid he'd punish them. Afraid he wouldn't. The nocturnal hitting happened during the twins' all-singing, all-tap-dancing, all-carousel-riding "we love you, daad-deee" period. He was clearly delighted with his matching blonde dolls. I was jealous as hell and afraid of losing him.

THE MIRACLE
INSIDE THE MADNESS

Watching Papp's face for signs of consciousness, I didn't hear Davy enter the room. "Lissa," he said softly, moving behind me, massaging my neck and shoulders. Grateful, I nuzzled his hand. Pappino moaned. Davy and I stopped all sound and motion. Papp opened his eyes. Not the wide-eyed stare. He simply opened his eyes and looked at us.

"Hello, Pappino. We've been waiting for you to wake up. We'll stay here, Davy and I, until you're strong and well. Do you understand that?"

He nodded.

"Do you know who we are, Papp?"

Pappino looked at Davy as if he, Davy, were retarded. He nodded emphatically. I looked over at his televised pine-tree heart show. It was a bit zigzaggy. I washed my hands in the tiny sink, then carefully placed my right hand over his left, not wishing to interfere with the I.V. needle that was deep in a vein of his right hand. He looked up at me. His eyes were eager.

"Easy, Pappino. Stay calm. Your heart is healing. It's . . . so good to see you." Knew better but couldn't help it. Tears came. No noise, just water. "I'm sorry, Papp. I'm just . . . seeing you see us. These are happy tears." I wiped my face, then wiped teary hands on my long black wool skirt.

"Now I have to wash my hands again." I did this quickly but thoroughly, then replaced my hand over his. He tried to speak, but the tubes in his mouth made it impossible.

"Don't try to talk, Pappino. Not with all that hardware in your mouth."

At the word "hardware," his eyes twinkled, and he made a breathy laugh-noise. Without taking my eyes from his, I spoke to Davy.

"Would you find Doctor Belliveau? If he's not here, please bring the cardio guy on duty."

"Right."

Pappino and I were in an eyelock belonging to every moment of every day of our shared life. My hand still rested atop his fingers. He pushed those fingers upward into my palm.

If you cry again now, I thought, you will sob your guts up. So I sang a dirty song: When I decided, as a teenager, to be a veterinarian, my father, at every one of my birthdays, sent me, along with more extravagant gifts, a song about animals. Some songs were happy, some sad. Many were quite beautiful. A few were completely filthy. Given how prone I felt to weeping, filthy seemed best:

Cats on the rooftops, cats in the aisles
Cats with the syph' an' cats with the piles
Cats with their arseholes wreathed in smiles . . .
As they revel in the joys of forni-CAYSHUN!

Papp breath-laughed, which made me both glad and worried; I didn't know how the mouth-tube worked in relation to the oxygen-prongs in his nose. Die laughing was the cliché. The expression had to come from somewhere.

His favourite animal-song, as sung by the younger me, was "All the Pretty Little Horses."

I began softly:

Hush-a-bye, don't you cry,
Go to sleepy, little baby.
When you wake, you shall have
All the pretty little horses.
Mares and bays, dapples and greys . . .

Davy and Dr. Belliveau were, finally, in the room.

"Look!" I whispered. Then louder, "Johnny Major is back amongst us."

Mareike was legendary for staying close to sources of current or potential income, so it seemed odd that she was not present. Perhaps this thought produced the life-affirming phrases that hit the three of us in the backs of our heads.

"There was never a divorce. Not even a legal separation."

All of us, including my intubated father, looked at her. She moved past us to the other side of the narrow bed and took his available hand, smiling at him.

"Please tell them, Johnny, was there ever a divorce?"

"Madame Major, this is not the time . . ."

"Yes, it is the time."

"As you see, he cannot speak, he . . ."

"He doesn't have to speak, Doctor. He can nod. Can you nod Johnny?"

Pappino nodded.

"Can you also shake your head for no?"

He nodded, then shook his head once from side-to side on the pillow.

"Mareike, please stop this . . ."

"No, Ellissa. Not until we all have the answer to one simple question. Johnny, were we ever divorced, or even legally separated?"

Pappino shook his head, as before, once, from side to side. Then he closed his eyes – not sleeping, not gone – simply reacting the way anyone did when confronted by Mareike's purity of focus.

Dr. Belliveau faced Mareike, then moved to stand as close to her as, earlier, Floris had stood to me. "Madame Major. Mister Major is having a significant rally. You. Can. Not! Trouble him with legal matters now. This room can only support two non-medical visitors at a time. I must ask you to wait outside."

Papp opened his eyes again, looked at me, seemed to be pleading. He then looked at Mareike, eyes narrowing. Fierce.

The joy, the love that had so suffused me when he opened his eyes in true contact, was seeping out into this battle. A battle I had known was coming. I wanted no part of it. The Johnny and Mareike Money War. I had managed, diligently, for as long as there'd been anything called Johnny and Mareike, to keep it out of my life.

In a closet-small, equipment-filled room containing a son, a daughter, a medical professional and a woman who would do absolutely anything in order to be the final recipient of the considerable accumulated wealth of a dying man, I knew that was all about to change.

"My father," I said softly, but with my version of fierce, "is not a lottery ticket."

Pappino squeezed his eyes shut. Water. I had, oh God, made him cry.

My hand still rested on his fingers.

"Pappino mio," I began in Sicilian. "You know how to fight this, but right now you must only fight to be well. When you are strong enough, you will tell me what to do about the greedy crazy people, and I will do it. Do you understand?"

He forced out a breath, pushing his lower lip and jaw forward, as much as he could with the feeding tube in his mouth. His eyes were clear. He pressed his fingers, hard, upward into my palm.

Dr. Belliveau clapped his hands for our attention.

"People. I must ask you to wait outside. Nurse Robitaille and I need to make Mister Major comfortable, to support his health. So, everyone, please, out now."

"It had to be dealt with, Ellissa dear."

"It did not have to be dealt with now."

"Yes it did. I knew you believed we were divorced. Johnny told me, a long time ago. He let everyone think this . . . unless they wanted to marry him. Then, he would tell them we were still married. He wanted it that way. For thirty years. It kept the gold diggers away from him."

"Except for you."

"That is uncalled for."

"Mareike. If what I've said were any more 'called for,' it would be a fucking petition!"

She moved to put her arm around me. I backed away.

"Do. Not. Touch. Me."

She backed away.

"Look, we're all tired and overwrought. It has been a complicated day. There is really nothing more I need to do here. And Count Brandoni is flying to Toronto to see a ballet. I promised to have dinner with him before he leaves. I will return to the hospital tomorrow. In the meantime, I think we should all get some rest, yes."

"No."

"Fine. Do what you think best, dear."

Scooping up her enormous fox fur, which had been lying on a chair like the round pile of dead animals it was, Mareike wrapped herself in it, pulled a dusty-pink knitted tam over whoever's hair she was wearing, and headed down the corridor to the lift. She pressed the button. The lift arrived. As the doors closed, she called out melodiously:

"Ellissa, dear, you should telephone Eddie Feinblatt."

COGNOSCENTI

I walked back to my hotel thinking about the Fierce Family Major. Why in hell did Mareike want me to call Eddie Feinblatt? I worked to fill myself with my father's history, as if it were the magic potion that would make me invincible. His power, I knew, belonged to the time Giovanni Paolo Maggiore became Johnny Major. It belonged to Cognoscenti.

A year after his wife's death, *Nonnu* Maggiore moved the family to Montréal.

I had liked *Nonnu* Maggiore. He was tall, thin and bald, with a long-toothed smile and pockets full of boiled sweets. When he visited us in England, he'd let me climb all over him, searching every pocket until I found every brightly wrapped sweet. He said I was *"una buonissima ragazzina"* because I always offered to share my treasure with him. I accepted his praise, never pointing out that it seemed only right to offer him some of his own candies.

When Pappino and I moved to London, *Nonnu* Maggiore chose to remain in Villa D'Agrigento, the Montréal apartment building that Papp owned, saying *"Montréale appartamento* is *la casa mia* now for a long time. My friends are here. We have *caffé* every day together. We eat together. I do not know *Londino."*

Nonnu died in his Montréal *casa* when I was ten – heart problems. My father accompanied his body to Sicily for burial. I was in the midst of exams at Peter Rabbit School and not allowed to go. Mammina came to London to stay with me but refused to stay in the Belgravia flat, even though Pappino was not there. She booked us into a suite at the Dorchester. We went to a Russian circus, to plays, films and flea markets. We played with dogs in Hyde Park. We ate in restaurants or, in matching terry robes, had crazy room-service meals that featured rich fancy cakes. She brought me back to the flat two hours before my father was due to return, and did not leave for the airport until he'd rung, saying he was about to take a taxi home.

"You're lucky, Ellissina. You have two parents who love you," she said before rubbing my cheek, attempting a hug and returning to her new family in British Columbia.

The Maggiore/Majors had been in business with the Feinblatts since before I was born – even before my father was out of his teens.

When *Nonnu* Nicu Maggiore became Nicholas Major, he needed a lawyer – all serious Canadian businessmen had lawyers. So *Nonnu* engaged Norton Feinblatt, who represented many Sicilian and Calabrian businesses in the neighbourhood. When "Old Nort" died, his son Eddie became my father's lawyer. His Canadian Barrister.

Nine years earlier, in Agrigento, Sicily, my father was born Giovanni Paolo Maggiore. His mother, my *Nonna* Maggiore, died of sudden heart failure three days after Papp's eighth birthday. Known to me only from a yellowed photo on my father's London bed-table, she had always been described as gentle, soft. I yearned for gentle, soft, but knew it would not likely be an option for some time to come. Instead, I had to be strong and determined, as Papp always described his father; had to be a fighter, as he always described my mother.

Mammina had been raised by nuns in a Taormina orphanage and never knew her parents. She believed her father was "still alive somewhere" but she didn't care "if or where he was living!" I remembered flinching, almost jumping, when she slammed the flat of her hand on the kitchen table and said, "He didn't want me when I was born. I don't want him now!"

Walking through the snow-covered Place Jacques Cartier, I wondered if this unknown grandfather could be living still. If not, was his death also cardio-related? A family of attacking hearts. It was a miracle, I thought, that my father was eighty-nine and still with us. *Nonnu* Maggiore wanted his two motherless children, particularly the boy, to have "good fortune with the English," so Nicu became Nicholas, and the family became Major. Then, at twenty-two, young John started becoming major.

He and two partners, Italian-Canadian friends from early childhood, opened Cognoscenti, a supper club where people ate fine food, followed by performances featuring some of the world's finest jazz and pop musical artists, and ballroom dancing to Billy Rand and his Famous Band.

At first, people couldn't pronounce the name. They'd say "Coggnosenti." Pappino's partners, Sal and Mauro, wanted to change it. As the majority shareholder, Papp said no. He said people would learn, said that if you gave them "something good. Something expensive and elegant, they will learn to pronounce the name. Cohn-yo-chenti. Pronouncing the name will make them feel expensive and elegant . . . it will make them . . . cognoscenti!"

People did learn to pronounce the name, and one club grew into three, the other two being in New York and Los Angeles. Pappino then bought out his partners and became sole owner. Sole *public* owner. The silent partners who gave him the money to start his business – more a consortium than any one individual – did not interfere very often. ("Occasionally, they'd push me to book somebody's girlfriend, or somebody's daughter's boyfriend. Then the *gavvone* would bomb and the profits would take a dive. After three or four of these, they got out of my way, let me do what I knew how to do. They were happy to do their other businesses, take a profit from mine, and have nice places to take their wives and girlfriends. And if I got into a jam they always backed me. When I got out of the jam I paid them back. Every penny. A good arrangement.")

My father married for the first time at thirty-eight. My mother was twenty-two. She was his only Italian marriage. I am his only dark-haired child. Both my parents say I have Pappino's hair.

At fifty-five, his thick, shiny, coal-black hair, "our" hair, started, slowly, to go grey. In the ten years that followed, it became a silvery mane. He said he'd had "good luck with the hair. Hair from my mother's family. My father had a billiard-ball head from the age of forty."

Finally in my hotel room, the feminised version of the Maggiore Family Face looked back at me from a gilded full-length mirror. At fifty, I too have the jet hair, with a few grey bits coming in at the temples. And the chocolate-brown almond-shaped eyes of my mother.

Could I, a private and quiet veterinarian, who'd built a calmer, less crowded and crazy life that I treasured – could I summon up the force of will to fight the fight that was building all around me? I asked the face in the mirror. That face looked back – silent, worried, and more than a bit scared.

FATHER, FARLEY AND THE FULL SLOPPY WOPPY

Thanks to my father and his father before him, Eddie Feinblatt was a rich man. With offices in both Montréal and London. Mareike was not the first person who had told me to call him.

Two years earlier, after his London cardiologist expressed concerns about "cholesterol. triglycerides and arrhythmia," Papp had driven from London to Southwold, needing, he said, "to heal myself spending a few quiet weeks with my Ellissina."

Despite being a thoroughly urban animal, Papp seemed happy hanging about at my small stone house, across the road from the animal clinic.

Having recently ended two simultaneous relationships (a one-year and a three-year), I too enjoyed the family closeness and male energy. I cooked. We ate. Some days, he'd come to the clinic to watch me work, playing with various cats and dogs. One of the dogs, a black Labrador Retriever called Farley, took a great liking to him. It was mutual.

"What's he in for, Farley?"

"A prophylaxis."

"A condom?"

"No, Papp. He's having tooth gunk removed. It only takes one session, but his humans are in Scotland visiting their son. They'll be back next week."

"He's a big dog. He should run. Would it be good if I exercised him?"

"Sure, as long as you don't tire yourself."

"Doctor said I should walk."

"Right. Dog runs, you walk."

So, every morning after breakfast, Papp would head out the door, grab a stick and fetch Farley, who would fetch the flung stick, over and over. I knew that most dogs were happy to fetch a stick all day. I did not know that my father would be happy to throw a stick all day.

It took a while for him to understand that the Lansdales, Farley's humans, shared his belief that "Farley is one great dog!" And that no sum of money would persuade them to part with their pet. "Oh come on, Ellissina. I really like that dog. He really likes me. The owners can name their price."

I sighed. "Pappino, how much would you take for me?"

"For you? You mean to sell you?"

"Right."

The dawn broke behind his eyes. "It's . . . like that?"

"Yes. It's like that."

I think he got it. Nonetheless, I was relieved when Farley went home, with my father not knowing where the Farley-family lived.

"I wish you'd told me when they were coming to get him. I would've liked to say goodbye."

"I said goodbye for you – I said 'Farley, my father – you know, that big good-looking stick-throwing guy with the great head of hair? He says goodbye.'"

"I'm serious."

"I know."

After each evening's meal, we'd sit by the fire in my wooden-beamed front room and listen to music. Papp loved the ballad singers of his youth – Frank Sinatra, Tony Bennett. Those voices, good as they were, had more to do with memories than music. The music that reached him, made him quiet and soft, was Baroque. Anything with lute or harpsichord was perfection. The Albinoni *Adagio* was best of all. As tough as he was, my father's musical core was a big, sloppy Southern Italian thing. As was mine.

One night, as we were being "post-prandial Albinoni sluts" (Davy's term), he said, very quietly, "When I die, everything goes to you."

I panicked (there is no more appropriate word for my reaction), grabbing his hand.

"Pappino. I don't want to talk about that. You've had . . . a minor . . . health scare. If you follow your doctor's advice, there is absolutely no reason to think about anything but being well and strong . . . and living."

"I understand, Ellissina, and I'm touched. But there are things you need to know. Trust fund provisions, pensions, insurance. The bulk of my money, and there's a lot . . ."

At that moment the damned *Adagio* did that swelling thing it does, which didn't help.

"Please, Pappino. I'm so glad you're here. I want us to be about life. Can we do that, please?"

He brought my hand to his face, covering it with his own hand. "You're the best. You and your brother. You two are . . . all there is. Okay, I'll stop. But I want you to promise me something."

"What?"

"If anything happens to me – and eventually something is going to happen to me – just call Eddie Feinblatt. He has all the details. Promise me you'll do that."

"I promise. Now I'm going to turn off the bloody Albinoni and put on English music hall songs. The only way to get us both out of Sloppy Woppy is a rousing chorus of 'When I'm Cleaning Windows!'"

EDDIE FEINBLATT

It was an unseasonably warm sunny Saturday morning. I didn't know whether Eddie Feinblatt was in Montréal or London, but assumed the family still lived in Westmount. I had that number.

Jason Feinblatt, whom I'd met as a newborn, sixteen years earlier, answered the phone.

"Hi, Jason. It's Ellissa Major, Johnny Major's daughter. How are you?"

"OK"

"Great. May I speak with your dad?"

"He's not here."

"Ah. Well, when do you expect him?

"I don't expect him . . . he doesn't live here anymore."

"I see. I'm sorry."

"No problem."

"Ah. Do you . . . have a number where I can reach him."

"He's at 767-0687"

"That's here in Montréal?"

"Yeah. Mount Royal."

"Right. Thanks."

I hung up, and dialed the number.

"Feinblatt here."

"Hi, Eddie. It's Ellissa Major."

"Ellissa. Good to hear your voice . . . I *have* been to the hospital to see your dad. Just before you came in from London. I understand he's doing better."

"Who told you? Mareike?"

"Yes, as a matter of fact."

"Well, she also told me to call you."

"Uh huh. She gave you this number, right?"

"No. I called the Westmount house. Spoke to Jason."

"It would be better if you didn't call the Westmount house, Ellissa. Things aren't . . . good there. I'm in the middle of a . . . difficult divorce. Johnny didn't tell you?'

"No, he didn't. I'm sorry, Eddie. I like Rachel."

"Yeah well, I don't like her very much at the moment . . . and she and the boys are pretty pissed at me."

"I had a sense of that from Jason."

"Oh? What did he say?"

"Just that you didn't live there anymore . . . but these things have . . . a sound."

"Yeah. I know. You've been through a lot of divorces. With Johnny, I mean."

"One fewer than I would've wished. Listen Eddie, Johnny wanted me to talk to you."

"Johnny did? I thought Mareike told you to call me."

"She did. But Johnny told me first. Two years ago. I know it's the weekend, but I wondered if we could . . ."

"Of course. Come to my office. I'm still in the same place. You remember where it is?"

"Across from the Ritz?"

"That's it. Say, in an hour?"

"Fine."

I opened the hotel window. Too warm for a down-filled coat. I put on the ancient toggle-buttoned tan anorak I usually wore to run across the road from my house to the animal clinic.

Since last I'd seen Eddie's building, it had been given an upmarket makeover. There was even a lift. Wanting exercise, I took the stairs.

Unlike his building, his office, my father, or my father's legal wife, Eddie Feinblatt had not been given a makeover. The sparse hair he had left was white, with a few strands combed across the top of his bald, liver-spot-dappled head. His basset hound face had further saddened with time; all jowly cheeks and a jawline collapsed into his neck. His smile and doggy brown eyes had retained the soft sweetness I remembered.

"Hello, kid," he said, coming around from behind his large oak desk and hugging me. He then backed up a bit, saying, "Well, well, well. You look good. Still have your dad's face, only prettier. And his hair."

"It's about the same length as his now. He liked it better long, but being a long-haired veterinarian is a nuisance. May I sit?"

"Sorry, kid. I must've been brung up in a barn, eh? Please sit." He gestured toward one of the burgundy leather chairs facing his desk.

"Eddie, Johnny is, I think – I hope – having a recovery. His cardiologist calls it 'a significant rally.' Mind you, at Johnny's age, I don't know exactly what that means.

"A couple of years ago, he made me promise that . . . if 'something happened' to him, I would contact you. I did not plan to do this contacting until he was . . . past saving. But, last night, Mareike told me they'd never been formally divorced. Which I did not know. Which, for his own reasons, my father had not told me. In my opinion, based on . . . various actions on her part, Mareike now feels herself to be . . . God, I hate discussing this! Anyway, she's acting like she thinks she is very close to – no pun intended – a major payoff. My father. Who, as I said, told me, without my asking, that if something happened to him, I was to call Eddie Feinblatt. About his will. Given how crazy things are going to get when and if . . ."

"There is no will, kid." I had to have heard that incorrectly.

"What?"

"No will. There is no will. There *was* a will. Then, four years ago, he took it back. Insisted on having all copies. He wanted to make some changes. In the course of doing all the other business we had together, I guess we both forgot about it."

"Forgot? About a document he believed to be there two years ago? My father? You know him, Eddie. If anyone, including you, or me, borrowed two dollars and fifty cents from him, and then, years later, returned two dollars, he'd telephone and say 'Where's my fifty cents?' Is this not true?"

"Yeah kid, it is. I don't know how this happened, I . . ."

"Right now I'd like a look at the other will, the one from four years ago."

"I don't have it. Johnny was adamant. He wanted *all* existing copies."

"I see. Do you . . . remember any of its . . . particulars? Beneficiaries?"

"Jeez, kid, I look at a lot of papers. I could be wrong, but I believe he left . . . the bulk of his estate to you . . . with some instructions for dispersal. Of course, I couldn't swear to that, not without the actual documents . . ."

"Of course. You're a lawyer. You couldn't swear to something without support documents."

I put my right hand over my mouth, then left hand over right. Sat there like that, just looking at Eddie Feinblatt, son of Morrie Feinblatt, my father's barrister and solicitor. He looked back, his doggy brown eyes sad but determined. A bit like a child's game, I thought – whoever looked away first was the weaker. Finally, I spoke: "Eddie. What you are telling me is that there is no will. Of any kind. From any time. None. Nothing."

"I haven't been able to find anything."

"Have you met with Mareike?"

"Yes. She also wanted to know about a will."

"I'm sure."

Eddie's face was still set, still resolute, but his eyes looked utterly miserable. "Look kid, I do have papers regarding the trust-fund money. For you, and for your brother. It's a sizeable sum. About a quarter-million for each of you. The mortgage is to be paid off on Mareike's Rome apartment. Nothing for her daughters, you know, the twins, and . . ."

"And everything else – his houses, the Cognoscenti buildings, all his belongings, his investments, other monies, all the rest of it . . . goes to his . . . legal wife, Mareike DeLyn Major?"

I'd always liked Eddie, in that way you like people who are extensions of your family. You like such people not for any particular trait (you don't usually know them that well). You like them because they are part of your family's team. What Pappino called "your backup."

I knew that my father, who trusted fewer than ten people in the world, trusted Eddie Feinblatt. And I knew for sure that Eddie Feinblatt had betrayed that trust. I let myself get really still and just think.

"No feelings," Pappino had said, fifteen years earlier, when Nick Brown left me, after almost five years together, with no explanation, no note, no anything. "When something bad happens, Ellissina," he'd said, "when somebody is playing games with you – a person, a group, a government – doesn't matter – when that happens, just go cold. Nothing's alive but you. You and your thoughts. If you do that, if you go completely cold, and just think, you will know what happened."

I did that. And I knew. "Big divorce, Eddie?"

"What?"

"Rachel is suing you for a lot, right?"

"What are you saying?"

"Nothing, Eddie. Simply asking a question."

I stood up and extended my hand. He shook it, watching me as if I were armed. Which I had indeed become. We both understood that.

"I'm sorry about this, Eddie. And I believe you are too. Thank you for taking time out of your weekend to tell me about the missing will. I need to decide what to do. Of course, if Johnny pulls through, which he very well can, he will . . . deal with this."

"Yes, I know that."

And I heard my father's voice again. "If you want something, if you need to have something, take your shot – whatever the odds, whatever the risks. It's what a brave man does."

"You're a brave man, Eddie."

For the first time in our meeting, Eddie Feinblatt looked terrified. I knew he would.

Go Cold, Get Cold

When I came out onto Sherbrooke Street, the weather had radically changed. Snow fell heavily, whirling in all directions at once – a proper Montréal snowstorm. My white trainers, anorak, as well as the black jeans, and white cotton turtleneck sweater under it, were far too light.

Nonetheless, I needed to walk. So, bare-headed, with anorak buttoned to the neck, and hands jammed into pockets, I did. Up to the top of Mount Royal, then back down to Ste. Catherine Street and south to my hotel in the cobblestone square of Place Jacques Cartier.

I rang Davy's room. No answer. Of course not, I thought, he's at the hospital.

It was my turn to take his place there, but, chilled and exhausted physically and mentally, I took the hottest bath possible, put on a white flannel nightie, got under the covers, and almost instantly fell asleep.

I awoke in the middle of the night – sneezing, leaky-nosed and a bit dizzy. I'd caught one helluva cold. For as long as I had that cold I couldn't go near my father.

"Hi, Lissa. It's me. Sorry for ringing you at sparrowfart, but I don't want to leave Papp's room until you get here, and . . ."

"I can't come to Papp's room, Davy. I've caught a huge cold. I need to talk to you. Call Auntie Nan and ask her to fill in for you. I'm sure she will. Alert the desk staff and the doctor on duty, and come to my room . . . Oh fuck, if you're going to be with Papp, I can't give you my cold! Look, get a mask and hospital gloves. Call me when you get to the hotel. I saw Eddie Feinblatt. I've important things to tell you."

"I have things to tell you as well."

"About Papp? Is he all right?"

"Yes, better and better. Still has a tube in his mouth, but he really wants to talk. He tried asking where . . . where the hell, in fact, you were."

"That sounds like Johnny Major getting well. What did you tell him?"

"I didn't want to say anything about you seeing Eddie Feinblatt. Didn't want to put him into business mode. Told him you were on your way. He's sleeping now. He still sleeps mostly. Which Doctor Belliveau says is necessary and good."

"Have Mareike or Floris been there?"

"No."

"Right. Their concerns . . . have been addressed."

"What do you mean?"

"Tell you when you get here. In the meantime, write a large-lettered note for Papp. Tell him you'll be back . . . before he misses you too much. Tell him I've got a monster cold and can't bring germs into his room. Tell him I love him and that I'll be there as soon as I'm de-germed, OK?"

"Will do."

"Don't forget the mask and gloves."

"Liss, I have to . . . Right. Mask and gloves."

There was a knock at my door. I expected room service with mint tea, honey and lemon. I got Davy. Maskless and gloveless. I sealed my mouth with my hand, and garbled: "I mu'n't beethe awn yu. Where yaw mas an' goves?'"

"It's all right, Lissa You can breathe on me. I have to leave this afternoon."

I dropped my hand and the germs did whatever they do. "What?!"

"May I come in and explain?"

He came in and explained. Two days prior to Auntie Nan summoning him from London he'd auditioned for the lead role in a kiddies telly show for the BBC. Tariq had been trying to contact him since the previous day. He finally called in for his messages, then tried to ring me, but I was out catching pneumonia. He'd got the telly job.

"It's a big, glitzy summer special. Three episodes. Decent money as well. If it gets developed as a series – even if it doesn't – it will give me terrific visibility. I have to take it. Papp would be the first to say that. In fact, he did. I told him as soon as I heard. He smiled, nodded, and said, twice, something that sounded like 'good.' Then he reached for my hand and squeezed it. You know Papp, Lissa. He loves it that we work."

Yes, I knew that. And I knew that Davy had to go to London and, possibly, become a kiddie-television star.

I also knew that Pappino had to get well if his life's work wasn't going to end as Mareike's Millions.

A MAJOR FAMILY DEITY

The Catholicism of both my parents was "lapsed" at best. Mine kicked in only at Christmas (couldn't quite get my mind around Easter – even veterinary medicine is science-based, and I was suspicious of rolling rocks and resurrection).

Nonetheless, in this life, sometimes somebody's God shows up. There we were, Davy and I, trying to figure how to build a retaining wall around our father when a Major Family Deity checked in, in the form of a telephone call from Auntie Nan.

"Ellissa?" she barked, in the smoker's cough that had been her voice for at least thirty-five years.

"Yes Auntie, it's me. I have a cold."

"I heard. Your mother's here. She's been here a coupl'a weeks, staying with me. Didn't want anyone to know. She's in with your father now. Speaking to him in dialect. He looks happy as hell."

This was really good news. I laughed and cried all at once. Then I was furious. "Damn!"

"What? Something gone wrong?"

"No, Davy. Things are going right. Righter and righter. But my parents, I love the pair of 'em, but they drive me crazy! They drive me totally spare! I've a father who does not tell me that he's never divorced the predatory barracuda of the world. I still don't understand why he, of all people, didn't protect himself, especially after his first heart warnings. And now I discover that my mother has been hiding out here in Montréal for weeks, without telling anyone but Auntie Nan. She, this mother of mine, is currently sitting in an intensive care room, making jokes in Sicilian with a man to whom she's refused to speak since I was a child. Secret-keepers. Southern Italian secret-keepers. They both think and act like Wop mobsters!"

"That, I take it, is the sort of thing you can say only if both your parents are Italian?"

"Right."

I then told Davy everything that had happened at Eddie Feinblatt's.

"What are we going to do now, Lissa?"

"Well, you are going to go to London and become the best beloved of Britain's *bambini* . . . and I . . . I am going to consult with the featherweight champion of the world."

"Who?"

"My mother."

After I blubbered countless germs all over Davy in the course of hugging, crying and saying goodbye, he left, and I sat cross-legged in the centre of my kingless king-sized bed, sniffling, snuffling and drinking mint tea.

WANTED, DEAD OR ALIVE

My father was getting well, but doing it in shark-infested waters. As had been true throughout our shared life, contact with The Shark sickened and tired me. This sickened exhaustion was intensified by The Core Problem. The Core Problem: Mareike, Floris and Petra wanted Johnny Major dead and I wanted him alive.

Actually, having neither seen nor spoken to Petra for some years, I had no idea what she wanted. Judging by Mareike's remarks at the hospital, Petra wanted the same thing from her mother and sister that I did – no contact. But what about our father? Did Petra think at all about money after his death?

Money after his death. What were *my* thoughts about money after his death? I'd never put the word "money" anywhere near the words "his death" – never let him speak of it, never let myself think about it, because any thoughts labelled Father's Death terrified me. I lived my own life, did my own work. Was so autonomous, so independent that men had left me because of it. Or too agreeably let me leave them. Only I knew that my ability to go forth in the world was because my father was in that same world. My independence was built on a dependency.

No matter how far away, no matter how out of actual contact, I knew Pappino would be there for me. That was all I needed. I did not need his money (though most people who say they would not like to inherit at least a cushioning sum of money – if only to distribute it where it is needed – are either lying or crazy).

Yes, I was appalled that this hard-earned and useful money could possibly be given to an essentially useless woman. That was disgusting, not frightening. I was an adult and a doctor: Dogs, cats, mothers and fathers all die. Everybody knows that, and so did I. But I was not just an adult, just a doctor. I was also a daughter. And the thing this daughter could not bear to think about was that her father would cease to be.

I knew how to work and how to live. I had friends, and, more often than not, lovers (most of whom I loved not deeply enough). I enjoyed my life, solving most problems as they arose. But, if I could not solve a problem, any problem at all – my father had always been there. Roof collapsing? Call Pappino. Relationship collapsing? Call Pappino.

"Go to Positano. I've a friend there, whose villa is empty, except for the servants. My friend, is here, in London, chasing some film actress. Let me arrange it. A few weeks away from where your guy's 'ghost' lives will help heal you."

Money problems? Borrow from Papp.

"You and your brother always pay me back. You two, and Mauro. Since Montréal, since the first Cognoscenti, you three always pay me back. So do most people, but I usually have to . . . remind them."

Actually, he reminded all of us, if we were even a few days late. He couldn't help it. Papp was a bean counter. That's how I knew there had to be a will, detailed down to the penny.

VANNI

As I continued bombing my cold with liquids and vitamins, I expected the next phone call to be from my mother. It was from my father.

"Ellissina? Good morning."

"Pappino?"

"You got it. They finally took the damn lead pipe outta my mouth."

"It isn't a lead pipe. It's a saliva absorption tube."

"Tube, my ass. If you had it in your mouth, God forbid, you'd call it a lead pipe too! You're my first call. You still have a cold?"

"It's almost gone, Papp. I'll ring Doctor Belliveau today to find out when I can return to you. I mustn't give you a cold . . . not when you're healing so beautifully."

"No cold, I understand . . . your mother wants the phone. Here."

"Hello, Ellissa."

"Hello, Mamma. Welcome to Montréal."

"*Grazie.* Listen, I spoke to Vanni's doctor. Nice man. He said I could visit you if we both wore these mask things. I have masks. I'm coming to your hotel as soon as Nanette gets here. Somebody has to stay here and deal with the Dutch bitch."

I heard my father laugh.

"Has she been there, the . . . Dutch bitch?"

"Not so far. Listen, when I leave Vanni here, I'll come to you. Wait in your room, OK?"

"Where am I going to go, Mamma?"

"I don't know where you're going to go. I'm just saying you should wait." Vanni. The last time I'd heard my father called Vanni I was three years old.

MY MOTHER THE BOLLARD

In England, they have round, hard grey concrete or black-brown bronzy steely things called bollards. Not very tall, but solid all the way through, bollards tell you that you cannot park somewhere, cannot drive through somewhere. I like the look of bollards – even when they interfere with the thing I wish to do. Unbreakable unmarked monuments. Rune stones without runes.

Everyone ages into something in addition to just an old human. Some become trees, others animals. My short, compact mother had aged into a bollard.

I opened the hotel-room door. There stood my matrilineal bollard, wearing a purple and yellow wool toque, around which curled tendrils of thick white hair. A red wool scarf was wound a number of times around her neck, but still hung almost to the hem of her emerald green down-filled coat. She was shod in heavy alpine boots with heels and soles that had, she said, the traction of tractors. This ensemble, startling on its own, was kicked into what Tariq, my brother's lover, called "The Salvador Dali School of Design" by a padded white hospital mask over her mouth and nose.

"Here. This other mask is for you."

"Hello, Mamma. Thank you. Come in," I replied, putting on my mask.

We two masked women made small talk as Mammina, whom I could no longer call Mammina ("It makes my two 'Doug-kids' feel left out. You can all call me Mamma"), unwound, uncoated, de-toqued and de-booted.

It was this last activity that opened my tenderness: my mother has small loveable high-arched feet with small loveable toes. My own feet are too big, my toes too long. I once declared to an entire class at Peter Rabbit School that "my mother has the most perfect feet in the world!" Those feet, clad in heavy black tights and pink woollen socks, dangled over the edge of my bed.

"Doug doesn't let me smoke. Can I smoke here?"

"No."

"Even a dog's doctor won't let me smoke."

"It's a non-smoking room, Mamma – nobody can smoke in it."

"You smoke?"

"No. That's why I asked for a non-smoking room."

"Is it a non-smoking balcony too?"

"Of course not."

"Fine. When I want to smoke, I'll go there."

"Fine. Do you want any food? Something to drink?"

"Booze?"

"Sure. If you want. Or coffee or tea."

"No. I want a hug."

So I hugged my mother the bollard, who immediately tensed up. She did not want a hug at all. I knew that. She always said she wanted a hug, because she thought mothers were supposed to want that from their children. She loved us. I knew that. She was simply not physical, unless it was about fighting or cooking. Perhaps, I thought, that was why my father had gone with other women so early in their marriage.

I told her all that had transpired with Eddie Feinblatt.

She listened intently, her almond-shaped spaniel-brown eyes shining above the hospital mask.

"Mauro," she said, when I'd finished. "Mauro Azzidone. Mauro might know where the hell Vanni's will is. Where is Mauro? Or Sal?"

"Sal died, Mamma. Last year. I didn't think to call Mauro. He and his third wife retired to Sardinia about ten years ago. I know how to reach him there. You're right. We should at least ask him."

"Third wife? Young?"

"Younger than Mauro. About fifty now."

The masked bollard started pacing back and forth in front of the bed. "Yeah, we'll call Mauro. And that woman who worked for Vanni for twenty years. Leora. Where is she now?"

"In London. They had a huge fight. About holiday pay. He was being impossible and she quit. I have her address and phone number."

"Good. We try her, we try Mauro. Fax their addresses and numbers to me."

"I can send an e-mail from the computer-room here at the hotel."

"No, fax. I make too many mistakes with the computer. Does anybody else know about the Feinblatt business? Besides the Dutch bitch?"

"Davy."

"Your brother Davy? The English?"

"The half English."

"Who told him?"

"I did."

"You shouldn't have. Don't tell anybody what you know."

I sighed. The other person who always said that, about practically anyone, was my father. Had he taught her that, or were they truly these two feudal *capi*, born knowing a pre-cognitive code? "Mamma, I trust Davy with everything. So does Pappino."

"Fine. But nobody else. Except Mauro . . . and maybe this Leora. Okay?"

"Fine . . . Mamma, I've got a question. Why did you come to see him, after over forty years?"

"Nanette phoned me again. She told me he said my name. A few times. In his sleep. She, Nanette, thought it could help him get better if he saw me. She told me about the Dutch bitch. I talked to Doug. He thought I should go. I thought, why shouldn't I go? Vanni's an old man. I knew you'd be here. He's been a good father. There are my reasons. I need a cigarette. Come to the balcony."

"Balcony's too cold for me right now. You go smoke. I'll wait."

It was still snowing. She put the entire colour festival back on and went out to the balcony, where she smoked and paced in the snow.

I waited. A cigarette's length gave her all the time she needed to get really angry. She stormed back in.

"That Dutch bitch! *Stronza*! Of all the dumb things he ever did, she is the worst!" Even muted by the muffling of a hospital mask, Mammina's anger was, as ever, a sizeable thing. I closed the balcony doors as she stomped about in my room, trailing snow onto the carpet. Outerwear was once again removed. This time, she sat in a chair. I resumed my cross-legged position in the middle of the bed.

"I know you love your father, Ellissina, but I'll tell you something. Something you probably already know, but don't like to think about. All his life, Vanni has been led around by his dick. His dick goes somewhere and he just follows it. This is true about most men. Not my Doug. Doug is not led around by his dick. That's because his people come from Scotland.

"But your father . . . it's like women with the big department stores. You know how the big department stores have cosmetics counters?"

"Yes."

"Well, at these cosmetics counters they give you all these little tubes of samples? Things to dry your skin, things to wet your skin; all kinds of things, you know?"

"Right."

"And these things, they're free. So you take them home. Even if your skin is already wet enough, already dry enough, you take the little samples home, because they're free. Well, your father, and most men, except maybe some of the ones whose people come from Scotland, they take sex from all kinds of stupid *stronze*. Why? Because it's free. If you're not in a whorehouse, the sex is free. But it is not free. You get old. You get sick. If the *stronze* are still alive, like the Dutch bitch, it costs you. And it costs your family. You see what I'm saying?"

"Yes, Mamma."

Mammina went on in this fashion for a while: Samples and *Stronze*. Non-Scottish men wandering the world, going wherever their penises pointed them. Then she put all her outerwear back on and gave me another wooden-soldier hug. At the door of my room, she said, "I go back to Vancouver tomorrow night. The day after tomorrow is Doug's birthday. He'll be seventy-six. It would be nice if you called."

"I will, Mamma."

She turned again to go, and again turned back to face me.

"Your father. Why I came here. I wanted to see him. OK?"

"OK."

She quickly kissed my neck, then crooked her index finger and rubbed my left cheek with it.

"I'll call you later. Or you call me. At Nanette's. OK?"

"OK."

Two minutes later, the phone rang. I thought Mammina'd either left something behind or forgotten to tell me something. It was Dr. Belliveau.

"Hello, Ellissa. How's your cold?"

I'd not sneezed for a while. My nose had stopped running. I wasn't dizzy and my voice sounded clear. I coughed. My throat was neither dry nor gunky with phlegm.

"Well, I feel just about better."

"Good. To be certain, wait until tomorrow before coming to the hospital. But I do need to speak with you. Could we meet at your hotel café in a half hour?"

"Sure."

Papp had started taking liquids and soft foods without a tube. His lungs were, "for a man his age, with his health profile," almost clear. Belliveau wanted to move him to "an interim recovery centre."

"It's a house, very nearby, maintained by the hospital. A full staff is on duty at all times with a decent amount of emergency equipment. If he relapses, he can be rushed back to Ste. Bernadette."

"Doctor Belliveau, he hates those places. Calls them 'temporary coffins with kitchens and crappers' or 'fleshbag hotels.' They frighten him. Couldn't we just take him to his Montréal flat? It has a lift – an elevator – he wouldn't have to walk."

"He's still pretty raw, Ellissa. He needs a round-the-clock nurse."

"We can hire a nurse. He has the money. He'll be in a place he knows, surrounded by his own things. He'll be happier, which will help him heal."

"Hmm. That might be possible. Let me think about it, yes?"

"All right. Please don't take to long. He's climbing back up. I don't want him frightened."

"I understand."

MAREIKE, SNAKE-WOMAN

That night I had The Dream. I'd had it many times – a few times a year, since I was seventeen and studying reptiles at the veterinary college.

In this dream I'm walking through a forest. I hear moaning and follow the sound. I discover Mareike and my father in a small clearing, between two trees. My father is sitting in a brightly coloured, finely woven Mexican hammock. I stand quietly behind a tree, watching them. They don't see me. Mareike is kneeling in front of the hammock. Like a snake, she is swallowing my father, feet first. She has swallowed him to the waist. This causes her body to bulge and become deformed. Pappino sits in his hammock, eyes closed, bare legs over Mareike's shoulders, pressing her to him with his heels, his toes arched upward. He is clearly enjoying the sensation of being swallowed by a wet mouth. Smiling goofily and half-dazed, he opens his eyes and stares at the top of Mareike's head. Her hair is Rapunzel-blonde. He reaches down to caress the long hair. It's a wig and comes off in his hands. He looks lovingly at the wig, then holds it to his face, smelling its perfume. I want to speak but no sound will come. Finally, I turn and run through the dense forest. Every time I have The Dream I wake up when I'm running.

I've always understood why I have this dream. The first time I saw Mareike, she had my father in her mouth, though not from toes-to-waist. Her back was to me. She was kneeling. I saw two naked heels; toes curled under, pressed into the soft white carpet, blonde hair and a peachy-white arse shaped like an upside-down heart. The hair was long, parted by bent-headedness just below her neck. Above the top of this blonde head were the chest, face and very surprised eyes of my naked father. Seeing me, he said "Oh God" and pushed hard at the pale shoulder of the hair-and-arse person, who fell away from him. Huge tits, I thought. He threw his burgundy silk dressing gown to her, then covered his penis with a bolster that looked like a larger penis of dark green satin with a golden tassel at each end.

The woman quickly wrapped herself in the dressing gown. Blotting her lips with the palm of her right hand, she stood up, smiling pleasantly.

"Ellissa," Pappino began hoarsely, "this is Miss Mareike DeLyn, a friend from Holland. Mareike, this is my daughter, Ellissa."

The woman, still smiling, walked towards me. "Hello, dear. It is lovely to meet you. Your father has told me so much about you. Would you like to join us for a bit of lunch?"

My father hasn't told me anything about you, I thought, disliking her instantly.

In fairness, it must be said that mid-blowjob is not a good time to meet a future stepmother. For a while, I tried to take this into consideration. I had come by without ringing. My father had a right to be fellated in his own flat, without first alerting the family. What worried me though, what put me off Mareike from the start, was that she'd been completely un-phased about being discovered, bare bum in the air, by the teenaged daughter of the man in her mouth. She was, I thought later, incapable of embarrassment. I remain convinced that this is the same as not having any awareness of, nor any interest in the feelings of others.

Seven months before the marriage, Mareike took to ringing me whenever she knew I was coming up to London (having asked Pappino for my number).

"Hello, Ellissa dear. Mareike here. Johnny says you're going visit us."

"Well, I will be visiting my father. If you're there . . . I shall see you then."

"Yes, of course. Actually, dear, I was wondering if you'd like to go shopping. I know many designers, and thought you might enjoy visiting their London ateliers. What do you think?"

I thought the idea of a designer-dressed veterinary student was giggle-making.

"I'm good for clothes, Mareike . . . but thanks for thinking of me."

"Of course, dear. Any time. I know young girls love clothes. My goodness, I'm not as young as you are and even I love clothes. I do suppose you'd rather see your daddy alone. Which is only natural. At any age. Perhaps we can all manage a meal together while you're here. I'll mention it to Johnny."

During a quiet dinner with Papp at his flat, I asked, "Is it serious with Mareike DeLyn? I mean, am I about to be a stepdaughter again?"

He smiled slightly, looking, atypically, a bit shy, running his hand through his hair, as he always did when he wanted a time-buy. "I dunno. Considering it. I do like her. She's fun. She knows people all over the world, speaks a number of languages . . . has interesting ideas. She . . . would you mind? If I married her?"

With his three other post-Mammina marriages, he'd always told me, never asked. Was that because I'd been too young for my opinion to be given full weight? Or, as I would wonder later, when Johnny and Mareike had gone to total ratshit, did he want to be talked out of it? Historically, nobody had ever talked Johnny Major out of something he'd decided to do. Had he been undecided? Whatever the case, all I said was, "You're a grown-up, Papp. You should do what you want to do."

"I know that, but I value your opinion. What do you think?"

I think she's bloodless.

I think she's cheap.

I think she's on the make for your money.

I think she's creepy.

Untrustworthy.

Dangerous.

Said none of that. Should have. Pure clumsy cowardice prevented me. Instead, I asked, "Do you love her?"

"Ah, 'love.' I'm not sure I've ever loved any of my wives . . . completely, except your mother. I've said 'I love you' to Mareike and she's said it to me. I think we probably both mean something more like 'I love being with you.' I do love being with her, and I'd like to stop running around. I think it's time to settle down. She's the person I'd like to settle down with."

"Well, that's it then."

Seven months later, John P. Major, of London and Montréal, and Mareike DeLyn, Dutch film star and Snake-Woman, were married on the middle floor of London Cognoscenti. Pappino wore an American-style tuxedo, shiny black shoes, white shirt, grey tie. Mareike's wedding ensemble was a very white, very fitted lightweight wool suit, with matching gardenias on her lapel and right wrist. There were hundreds in attendance. Years later, Davy would describe the makeshift aisle-and-vicar rearrangement of the restaurant as "a charming nuptuality, taking place at Our Lady of the Crap Table, a wee gamblers' church in Central London." At age twelve, however, he just whispered, excitedly, "White! She's in white! Isn't white for . . . ?"

"Mm hm. Virgins . . . and Dutch actresses."

"Do those two things . . . usually go together?"

"Virgins and Dutch actresses? Probably not in most cases. Definitely not in this one."

ELLISSA AND ELISA

In Montréal at mid-afternoon, certain I was cold free, I returned to Ste. Bernadette Hospital. Snow was coming down hard, but this time I was ready for it: Black Sorel boots, wool toque, scarf, gloves and ankle-length down-filled quilted coat. To be super safe, I wrapped a mask in an unused guest-towel and bunged it into my handbag.

The day was sunny and the snowfall was, as it always had been for me, purifying, focusing. I would use that pure focus to help heal my father.

Who was not in his room.

The nurse on duty said he'd been moved.

"Moved? To another floor?"

"No. To the Recovery Centre."

"Recovery Centre? He can't be moved without me agreeing. I'm his daughter. I had to be notified . . ."

"I dunno, ma'am. My shift just started. You should check with Doctor Kingsley."

"Who in hell is Doctor Kingsley? Where is Doctor Belliveau?"

"On vacation."

"Vacation? That's not possible. I spoke to him yesterday."

"Well, he must have started vacation after his shift this morning. See, it says here *'En vacance, jus'qu'a* 14/1/2002.'"

She was so calm. She did not have a vanished father!

"Look, this can't be happening! Doctor Belliveau would have mentioned . . . Oh God, where is this recovery centre?"

"Three blocks away. At our transition house. Ten-twenty-nine rue St. Antoine. 'Ste. Bernadette Maison de Récuperation.'"

"And where exactly is this Doctor . . . Kingsley?"

"He's here. I'm Doctor Kingsley," a voice said from behind me.

I turned. Short, slope-shouldered, potbellied. Curly red-brown hair streaked with grey, scalp showing through. A cherubic Santa's workshop face, or so I would think later, when I was something other than borderline berserk. He smiled. Which, under the circumstances, infuriated me. What are you grinning at, you stupid bugger? I thought. My father has vanished!

"Where is my father?"

"As you've heard, Missus Major . . ."

"I am not 'Missus Major.' I am one of the few people on earth who is *not* Missus Major. I am *Doctor* Major, *Miss*. Doctor Major, *Mizz* Doctor Major. The daughter. The one who must agree to sign him out. Mrs. Major, at least one of the Mrs. Majors, is a homicidal greedhead who has actually tried to kill my father, in full view of Doctor Belliveau, which we can't prove but which we all know to be somewhere between highly probable and absolutely certain! Which is why Doctor Belliveau signed a document saying that my father could not be moved without written agreement by my brother or myself!"

"I see. Why don't we go downstairs and find out when your father *was* moved. Would you like to do that?"

"Doctor Kingsley, please don't speak to me as if I were gaga. I am not gaga. I simply wish to know . . ."

"Where your father is and when he was taken there, yes?"

"Yes."

"Fine. Please follow me."

The sign-out woman said my father had been moved to the Recovery Centre "less than a half hour ago," and that his daughter had signed. She showed me the signature. "Elisa Major." One 'l.' One 's.'

"How do I get to this Recovery Centre?"

"Out the door. Turn right. Two blocks. Turn left."

I took off.

FIERCE FALLS

"I'm here to see my father. It's urgent. His name is John Major. I'm his daughter. Ellissa Major."

"Really? That's odd. There is another Ellissa Major inside with her father."

"There is no other Ellissa Major! Just me! I am the only Ellissa Major!"

The woman was being, as Dr. Kingsley had been, sweetly reasonable. I was being, I knew, wild-eyed and crazed. I was certain, however, that I was Ellissa Major. To verify this, I proceeded to pull out credit cards, health cards, driving licence and my discount card from Boots Chemists.

The woman at the desk of the Ste. Bernadette Maison de Récuperation nodded. She may well have thought Ellissa Major was crazy, but I could see her accept that, at the very least, I was Crazy Ellissa Major.

"He, your father, is in the Sun Room."

"Sun Room?" I shouted, pointing. "Look out that window! It's dusk! There's no sun out there!"

"It's called the Sun Room regardless of the time of day."

And because this was funny, at any time of day, I laughed. And she, bless her, seeing the joke, laughed too.

The laughter reduced my manic hysteria. Still urgent, but no longer wild-eyed, I asked, "Where is he? Can you take me to him now?"

I replaced my identification cards and then the woman walked me briskly to the Sun Room.

The room, a round, mostly glass solarium, was ringed with very old men and women. Some looked all right – alert, engaged, alive. Most, however – in chairs, in wheelchairs, propped onto Zimmer frames, lying on cots – were vacant-eyed and slack-jawed. Residents of the Fleshbag Hotel. I knew that was how they appeared to my father, how they appeared to me.

In the middle of this aggregate of moaning, murmuring, muttering, shaking, gurgling, drooling and wall-eyed staring, was Pappino. Strapped into a wheelchair. "'Up!" He was rasping. "Up! Out!'" He saw me. His eyes filled with tears.

"Ellissina. Up! Out! I am! Not! This!"

I knelt at his feet, trying to unstrap his legs. We were both crying noiselessly. My tears fell onto his black velvet monogrammed slippers. "No, Pappino. You are not this. There's been a mistake. I'm gonna take you home now."

"Yes! Home! Now!"

As I began to untether my father, the nurse, a large woman, clamped down on my shoulder. In the way that people, *in extremis*, can lift cars off their bodies, I shook her off. She said, "Missus Major, you cannot . . ." and ran from the room, shouting urgent words in an urgent tone.

I quickly unbuckled Pappino's foot-straps, and then the one around his chest. Pushing with both arms, he stood up, jutted out his jaw and fell like a tree, face down.

I turned him over. Blood ran from his nostrils into his ears. I screamed for someone to "please, please help! My father has passed out!"

Two men came immediately, pushing a gurney. One took Pappino's pulse, said he was "gone."

"No – not gone. He's lost consciousness. Please! Please! We have to revive him. He will revive! We have to try! He's very strong, he will . . ."

One of the men, tall, black, with large hands, held me gently but firmly by both my upper arms. "Easy," he said. "We'll take him into the other room. We'll do what we can."

"I'll go with you. I'm his daughter."

He was dead, had been dead from the moment he hit the ground. Not temporarily, revivably dead. Fully and irretrievably dead.

John the paramedic ("That's his name too. My father. John.") sat me in a chair and brought me a paper cup filled with of water. Bone dry, I drank it in a gulp and then crumpled the cup into a ball. Rolling the paper ball in my left hand was comforting. I could feel my Bastina-self coming through to protect me from panic. I was calm. Not crying, not screaming. My eyes felt bugged-out but they were dry.

"They're gonna take him back, in an ambulance, to the hospital."

"Can't he stay here? Just for an hour. I must figure out . . . what needs to be done?"

"It's a health law. He needs to be in . . . a cold room. It's better for *him* that way too. You don't have to do anything until tomorrow morning."

"Yes. Yes, I do. There's a woman, his . . . oh, it's too complicated. He, my father, still needs my protection."

"He'll be safe at the hospital. No one can do anything about him, or to him, until tomorrow."

"Are you sure?"

"Totally."

And because I needed to, I believed him.

I had to sign a paper saying I'd unbuckled him. I inserted the words "at his urgent and definite demand" and signed. Daughter Elisa Major (one 'l', one 's'), who'd brought him there, had to sign a release form, so that Paramedic John could take Father John to a cold room. As the only Ellissa Major (two 'l's, two 's's) available, I signed that paper as well.

"This other Ellissa Major, where is she now?"

"I don't know. I looked around for her while you were . . . bent over your father. It's weird. She was there one minute, and flat gone the next."

"What did she look like?"

"Blonde. About your height. Skinny. Superskinny, with really big eyes."

PETRA

She wore a hooded pale pink quilted bomber jacket, heavy woollen black leggings, pale pink wool gloves, a matching scarf, and white moon boots. Standing just outside the building under a streetlamp, she wanted to be seen.

"Hello, Petra."

"Hello, Ellissa."

Her voice had grown up to be low and sultry, an agreeable sound. Her thighs were thin as upper arms, her face a skull. A skull with the cupid's bow mouth I remembered from her childhood, prominent cheekbones, and a shock of butter-blonde hair that fell in front of her huge eyes – round blue eyes. Her sister's eyes – her mother's eyes.

Night had come. Snow was still falling, a soft and crunchy white carpet underfoot, up to the ankles of my boots.

"Is Papa all right?"

"He's dead."

"He was alive when I brought him there. Brought him there so we could talk. We were talking. First time in many years. Then I saw you walking toward the room. I got scared. I ran away. I did not kill him."

"Yes, Petra, you did. Bringing him to that place killed him. You brought him to that place."

"I wanted to talk to him. Without Mama. Without Floris. Without you."

"Whatever you wanted, your bringing him there killed him."

"If that's what you think, there's nothing I can say. I should go, yah?"

"That's your decision."

She shook her head, hard. "I did not kill him. Did. Not."

She turned and started towards Ste. Catherine Street. Kill, I thought. Kill means dead. Dead Father. Dead John Major. Dead Pappino. Alone, me. Sister. Half-sister. Same father. Walking away. Alone me. No.

"Petra!"

She turned.

"Wait!"

She continued to face me, not moving towards me, not moving away. Petra, perfectly still in the falling snow, standing in front of Dépanneur Désbiens. Then she shouted, "I'm going in here! For cigarettes!" I could see her doing her transaction, blurry in the heat-misted window of the dépanneur. Cigarettes acquired, she opened the door and stood in the snow, looking at me with large, seemingly opinionless eyes.

"You smoke, Ellissa?"

"No. Stopped years ago."

"Mind if I do?"

"Not outside."

"You mind inside?"

"I don't care. I want a drink. You want a drink?"

"You drink?"

"Not a lot. I'd like to now."

"Yah. Me too. You buying?"

Don't bust my chops. That's what . . . he would say. Don't work me. Do you know, Petra, that I cannot let . . . his . . . leaving in yet? Do you know that if I start to cry now I will lose control? Do you know, Petra, that if I start to cry now I will wail the world down? You *do* know, Petra, that I don't want to be alone. I can see you knowing this. You know I'm begging. I can beg, but I will not grovel. I know the difference.

"I can buy. It's your first trip to Montréal in . . ."

"Twenty years."

"Right. So I'll buy."

"*Danke*. If you come to Amsterdam, I will buy you a drink. And give you a joint. You smoke dope?"

"No."

"Good. More for me. So, where do we drink?"

"Around the corner. Bistrot Claudine."

Sitting across the booth from me, Petra looked like a gaunt, tougher version of the little girl I'd known in Belgravia. The one who, on command from her sister, would hit me at night. As I had done then, I stared in wonder at her blonde hair. I had seen this blue eyed blondeness, as did most dark-haired British girl-children, as a mark of privilege, of a higher caste. I had envied it. As a long-time dark-haired Briton – British, but not English, I probably still did.

Once settled into our booth Petra removed her parka, scarf and gloves, revealing a clingy pale grey cashmere pullover, sleeves fashionably overlong, covering her hands to just above the knuckles. I did not envy her anorectic body, ribs visible through the cashmere. A flat-chested nippled twig, evoking pictures of the world's refugee colonies and work camps. The prettiest of the damn near dead blonde Bosnian Muslims behind the barbed wire. She smoked, inhaling deeply, which thrust her cheekbones further forward. Perhaps out of undeclared thoughtfulness, she blew the smoke out through her nose, sending it downward, rather than across the booth into my face.

"Mama left all these messages on my answering machine. 'Your father is dying in Montréal.' She named the hospital. She said it would be 'smart,' that was the word she used, 'smart,' for me to be there. 'At his bedside,' she said.

"I had no intention of going to Daddy's smart bedside. Why would I? For years, lots of years, he refused to speak to me, to take my calls, to answer my letters. Every four months I got a cheque from some solicitor's office in London. Feinblatt and Feinblatt. No personal letter. Not even a scribbled note. Just this cheque. Five years ago, creating and teaching art were making me enough money, so I sent the cheque back, with a note saying I was supporting myself with my work, with my art. It felt really good to do that. I sent the next cheque back as well. Also with a note. He did not reply, did not acknowledge that I was no longer accepting his money.

"The cheques stopped coming. I suppose that was his acknowledgement. I tried ringing him again. He took the call . . . but was so cold. Hello. How are you? What do you want? I said I didn't want anything. Just to say hello. And to invite him to an opening I was having in London. There was a silence. I thought he'd rung off. He'd done that to me before. No goodbye, just a dead phone.

"Then finally, he said, 'I think it would be best if we left things as they are. If you need money for housing or food or medical bills, let Feinblatt's London office know.'

"'You're my father.' I said. Not loud, just 'You're my father.' 'I know,' he said, 'that's why you can always call Feinblatt if you want for . . . any necessities.' I rang off. The way he used to do to me, without a goodbye or anything. If I did not ring off, I was going to start screaming 'You're a heartless bastard! You're a shit!' Screaming that I was not my mother, not my sister. That I was a separate person. A person he once said he loved, adored – he would hold me in the air, flying me around. Saying 'You are my adorable Petra! and I adore you!' It was one of the first English words I learned, 'adore.'"

"Yes. He said that, he did that with . . . all of us."

"Well, he stopped doing it with me. Completely stopped. With no warning. Because of my mother and sister. I had done nothing bad! Nothing . . . except be related to Mama and Floris, I, I . . ."

She began crying. No sound, just tears rolling down over her cheekbones and onto her pullover, making tiny charcoal coloured circles on the light grey wool. She stubbed out her cigarette, took a paper serviette from the holder on the table, wiped her eyes, then held the crumpled paper in her fist, which had come to rest on the tabletop. I put my hand over the fist. She sniffled and sighed, but did not with-draw her hand.

We sat that way for minutes, each using our free hand to drink beer from a bottle. She was looking down into her lap, and then looked up at me. Gone was the neutral, open gaze. Her eyes were softer than the hole-burning Sicilian brown that connected the eyes of my mother, my father, and me. Petra's eyes weren't Mareike's cunning advantage-evaluating surgically wide eyes. They were a black-flecked baby blue version of the Fierce Family Major. Our father, pushing his southern Italian spirit through the Dutchness.

"Sorry about the tears, Ellissa. I will change the subject. I'm going to be part of a group show in New York – a piece from my 'Bird/House' series – a stuffed taxidermy bird inside a dollhouse – so I decided to stop in Montréal to try and see my father. Not because it was Mama's idea of 'smart.' In fact, Ellissa, I would appreciate it if you don't men-tion to Mama that I was here, that you've seen me. I'm not going to contact her. Mama and Floris are . . . not part of my life anymore. I am here simply because I wanted to try, perhaps for the last time, to con-nect with my father. So I went to the hospital. When I got there, Daddy was on a stretcher next to the reception desk. He was drugged. They were taking him someplace. I said I was his daughter, which I am. They said 'Ellissa Major?' I thought 'yes' was the right answer. I said yes. They asked where I lived. I said in the U.K. My accent was right. Every-one who learns English in Europe learns British English. They asked for my, for your middle name. 'Giovanna,' I said . . ."

"You remembered that?"

"I remember everything about you from when I was a child. You looked like him and he loved you. He never stopped loving you. He never threw you out of his house, which you thought was your home. He never cut you out of his life. You saw him all the time. I wanted to be you . . ."

"So, you signed him out of the hospital?"

"Yes, and I rode in the ambulance. Sat on a bench, next to the good-looking black guy."

"John."

"Yes. John. Same name as Daddy. Daddy's face looked beautiful in sleep. That big head. I didn't know what would happen if he woke up and saw me. Didn't know if he'd even recognise me. I did think that if he woke up and was angry that I was there, it could kill him. I did not want that. Which surprised me. I did not want to kill him, did not want him to die. I wanted . . . this impossible thing. I wanted him to see me, to know me, and to be glad I was there.

"When we got to the old people's home, he began to wake. They strapped him into a wheelchair. I signed for him, with your name, and they wheeled him into this round glass room. I went to the room; it was filled with . . . living dead people. Daddy was wheeling around and around, looking at these . . . these ancient skin-covered skeletons, and totally freaking out."

"Petra – until he saw those people, he didn't know he was old. Older, yes, but not old. Old had never occurred to him."

"And there it was?"

"And there it was."

"That's what you meant when you said I killed him?"

"Yes."

"I didn't mean to."

"I know."

I squeezed her still-fisted hand. I wanted to hold her, wanted to be held by her, but we were separated by a table, and by much else. Things that I would not, could not, let in. Not while I needed to take care of the man who had taken care of me. Vigilance was still very much required. Would it always be?

Petra extracted her hand from under mine, took a deep drag on her cigarette, exhaled, then swallowed the last of her beer. She stood, putting on her parka. "I'm glad we got to visit. I'm sorry Daddy is dead."

The avoided subject. The huge thing with which I would be left alone when she went away. "I know, Petra. But thank you for saying it. Where are you headed now?"

"To my motel, next to the airport. My flight is in early morning."

I stood. "Why don't we walk together to my hotel? It isn't far, in Old Montréal. You can get a taxi there, or an airport bus. It's a pretty part of town, in the port, with cobblestone streets."

She smiled. A shy tight smile – almost an experiment. "Yes, I would like to see your 'Old Montréal.'"

"You know you've been here before, Petra. When you were a child."

"Yah. When Mama and Daddy were together. Mama just wanted to shop for clothing and eat in fancy places. We saw only shops and restaurants.

"Yesterday I walked a lot. I like this place. Grey stones with many green spires. And those crazy curly outdoor metal stairs on the houses. Quebec French is different to what I know. Hard for my European ears to understand. But I can do it if I listen hard. Montréal is like a small Europe. Like Paris mixed with Prague."

I was still avoiding the full weight of Dead Father. There was delay offered by leaning into something simpler. I let myself lean into the picture of two sisters walking in the snow, sharing a city.

The snow had stopped while we were in Bistrot Claudine. The white-blanketed Place Jacques Cartier looked like a Québécois Christmas card.

"Wow! This neighbourhood looks like a fairy tale!"

"Our brother Davy, says it looks like a film set."

"Davy! I've not seen him since . . . do you see him?"

"Yes. He lives in London. He's an actor."

She laughed lightly, placing a pink-gloved hand to her chest.

"Yes, I knew. An actor. Two of us making art. I like this! We . . . we know so little of each other. I am sometimes in London. Do you think he'd see me?"

"I'm sure he'd love to see you, Petra." She pulled a pen and a little notepad from an inside pocket. "Does he have an e-mail address?"

"He does."

"Do you think he'd object to my having it?"

"I . . . don't know. I should check with him first."

"Of course."

Her face took on that tough, closed look. The one I'd seen when she'd thought I wouldn't speak with her, when she'd turned to buy cigarettes.

"I'm sure Davy will be pleased to give you his e-mail, Petra. It's only that we promised each other to always check, before . . ."

"I understand. You should do that, you should check. And you? Do you have an e-mail address?"

A corner, with me backed into it. A test. I wanted to pass this test.

"Yes. It's 'major_petvet@angliafile.com.'"

"Want mine?"

"Yes, of course."

She scribbled her e-mail address, tore out the tiny piece of paper, and handed it to me. It read "Petrel@Amnet.ne."

"Petrel. That's a bird."

"You know this bird?"

"Southwold, where I live, is on the sea. The Petrel is a sea bird. Quite small. Southwold bird-watchers call Petrels accidentals."

"Accidentals? Why?"

"They're not native to England, but because we are on the sea – they fly into our area by chance. Such birds are called accidentals."

We stood there, suddenly awkward – two intimate strangers.

"Accidentals. Yah. Accidentals."

"They are lovely birds, Petra."

"Yes they are. Ellissa. Please don't mention to Mama that you've seen me. I'm not going to contact her. She left all these messages on my Amsterdam machine, but she and Floris are no longer part of my life."

"I won't. I promise."

I hugged her, and was hugged in return. She was so thin.

She gently pulled away, looking at me.

"You think I should eat, right?"

"It's not my place to tell you . . . but yes Petra, I think you should eat."

"It's all right. Everybody thinks I should eat. Don't worry. I'm quite strong. I go to the gym almost every day. And I eat enough to live. I will eat more when . . . when I want to live more . . . and when . . . Ellissa, would you like to come to the group show? In New York?"

"Of course I would. I don't know if I can. There's so much to do here, and . . ."

"This is very big for you. You and Daddy were so close. You are new to losing him. I've been losing him for many years . . . Look, here's a flyer for the show. On the bottom is the telephone number where I will stay. If you can make it, great. If not, there will be other shows."

She flipped the palm of her hand up in a frozen wave, smiled slightly, lips closed, then turned and, like a whippet, ran across the road and climbed into a taxi. The taxi headed up Place Jacques Cartier, leaving me alone.

SIBLINGS

"Davy . . . I know it's the middle of the night . . ."

"Lissa . . . is it Papp? Is he . . . ?"

"Yes."

"When?"

"Earlier tonight. Heart gave out."

"Mareike involved?"

"No, actually. But, as his 'legal wife' in the wild and will-less world, she will very likely be up to her arse in involvement by morning. Papp's body is . . . on ice at the hospital until then. I need to be there tomorrow, I need to . . ."

"How are you holding up, Lissa?"

"I'm sort of numb. Haven't let myself look at it yet. And I haven't been alone. I just left Petra."

"Petrified?"

"No, Davy, not 'Petrified' any more. Just 'Petra.' I'll tell you . . . when I see you . . . I'm pretty knackered . . ."

"Is she thin as a broom-handle? I'd heard she was."

"She's very thin. Too thin – she does artwork. Seems to be having shows all over the place."

"Yeah, there've been a few in London. Saw the name 'Petra Major' in *Time Out* two years ago. Tariq and I went. She wasn't there. Her work's good, if a bit creepy. Dead birds."

"Always dead birds? I didn't . . . she asked about you. Was so pleased that you're an actor; 'two Major children making art!' she said. She wanted your e-mail. May I give it to her, the next time we're in contact?"

"Fine. It would be interesting to see old Petrif . . . Petra again. I only knew her as a child, as one half of Mareike's Dancing Dollies."

"Be kind to her if she sends an 'e', Davy. What with Mareike, Floris . . . and Papp, for that matter, her family life has been pretty rotten."

"Yeah, okay, but right now it's you I'm worried about."

"I'll be all right. There's lots to do. I don't have time to lose it."

"You sound like Papp."

"Yeah, well, somebody has to."

MAREIKE AND HER DAUGHTERS

Pappino's death made the papers in French and English, with a ten-year-old photo of "Montréal Entrepreneur and Jet Setter, John Major," and a forty-year-old publicity shot of Mareike from *Haunted Holiday:*

Montréal entrepreneur, John Major, 89 (born Giovanni Paolo Maggiore, in Agrigento, Sicily), creator of the exclusive and expensive "Cognoscenti" clubs and casinos (Montréal, New York, Los Angeles, London), died last night, of congestive heart failure, at the Centre de récuperation of Ste. Bernadette Hospital.

Major, known as both a successful businessman and an international playboy, married five times, and fathered four children. His widow, the former Dutch film actress, Mareike DeLyn Major, had been keeping a vigil at his bedside, along with one of their twin daughters, Ms. Floris Major, as well as Ms. Ellissa Major, Mr. Major's daughter by his first marriage to the present Mrs. Ellissa Robertson of Victoria, British Columbia.

John David Major, Mr. Major's son by BBC newscaster Jennifer Applewhite, had also been at his ailing father's side (as, briefly, had Ms. Applewhite), but has returned to England to film the children's television special "Jimmy JollyJumper," in which he plays the title role.

When contacted last night at the Hotel Vogue, Mrs. Mareike DeLyn Major said, 'I will take Johnny's body back to Sicily. He wished to be buried there, alongside his parents. He was a remarkable man, a rags-to-riches success story. Johnny could not live all the time with only one woman, but we remained very close until his death. His passing is a very great loss.'

And, in the seeming absence of a will, a very great gain, you lying, bogus, slapper, slag-slut-bitch, *stronza*, I thought, with what I believed to be uncharacteristic vulgarity.

Heading to Ste. Bernadette's morgue – the cold room – I thought about the American Atomic Bomb Man. The Manhattan Project man. Oppenheimer. When he made the bomb, he is reputed to have said, "I am become death." Davy had said, on the phone, that I sounded like Papp. In the early morning dead-father fluorescence of the hospital, at least with regard to my language choices, I had also become my mother. I had become a pair of angry, untrusting, vengeance-seeking Sicilians. I knew I could never be as powerful as either of my parents, but I was reaching hard to hold them in front of me. My shield. As Pappino used to say when he sent me off to Peter Rabbit School, "Return with your shield and not upon it."

"Morgue-Salle Cryonique," it said on the door. Pain and pun are almost the same word. "Pappsicle," I thought.

"Something is funny, dear?" Mareike asked.

"No, no, just nervousness. Sorry."

"Of course, dear. This must be very difficult for you. It is . . . a difficult time for all of us."

"I'm sure." I tried to smile. Couldn't. Could hear how hostile I sounded. So be it, I thought. Relative to my rage and pain, I was a summer's day. Did what I always do when seeking an alternative to telling Mareike to please fuck off and die – studied her makeup and wardrobe.

The usual can-be-seen-from-the-next-county Hollywood makeup. Black silk sheath suit. Black snakeskin sling-back shoes. A tightly fitted 1940's-style black turban with a gold circle pin in the centre. Her accessories included tiny gold hoop earrings, a topaz ring and Eddie Feinblatt.

Mr. Feinblatt, barrister and solicitor, wore a rumpled dark blue suit and slightly crooked yellow tie. Slightly crooked and yellow. Just like Eddie. Exactly what Pappino would've thought, had he lived to think it. I giggled again.

"Sorry – giggling sometimes happens to me when – things are, as you would say, Mareike, very difficult. Hello, Eddie. Are you here representing my father's interests?"

"Not exactly, dear. As the executrix of Johnny's estate, I have retained Eddie's services."

"Isn't that a conflict, Mareike? Eddie, as did his father before him, represented my father."

Eddie, who'd been softly clearing his throat, and avoiding my eyes, now looked at me. Sort of. He focused his gaze on a place just to the left of my left eye. "I would certainly be representing Johnny, Ellissa . . . if he were alive."

"Which, sadly, he is not, dear."

"And," Eddie continued, "I will, naturally, represent Johnny's interests when and if there is business relating to pre-mortem documents."

"Such as a will."

"Which there is not, dear."

"Which is amazing."

"Which is . . . surprising."

"There are, of course, the trust fund items . . ."

This scavenger hunt outside the Morgue-Salle Cryonique (with at least one scavenger in attendance) was interrupted by the running entrance of Floris, startlingly enrobed in an ankle-length tent-thing, silver leaves on a black background, from under which there peeped the pointy toes of black and silver cowboy boots.

Oh Davy, I thought, this fashion parade would be such fun for you and Tariq, which in turn would be a huge help to me.

"Sorry, Mama, sorry I'm late. Petra called again and . . ."

"Petra called me, dear? That seems impossible. I'd given up hope of ever hearing from her."

"But she called last night, Mama, after she came by for the papers and . . ."

"After I went out to dinner? Really? I'm so sorry to have missed her, and missed her call. Why didn't you tell me, Floris? Did she leave a message?"

"But you spoke . . . message? I . . . yes, message. She said she'd . . . call again today. Which she did. Today. Again. Which is why I'm late."

"Ah. That's fine, Floris. Not to worry. Did you tell her to call this afternoon? After three?"

"Yes. She said she would do that." Floris then tapped at her upper lip, as always, three times, with the three fingers of her right hand. Bad Floris. Bad, cover-blowing Floris.

Oh Pappino, oh Mammina, I thought. I've been fit up. I've been fully and completely had. By Petrified, the Bird Girl. Who was working for her mother all along. Fuckin' 'ell! I am so entirely nowhere near as good at this shit as either of you. And I never will be.

"Do you want to go inside the Salle Cryonique, dear? To see your father . . . one last time."

My voice was low and precise. "I have seen him, Mareike. I have seen him all my life. And I will see him for the rest of my life. I do not wish to go into that room. I read in this morning's paper that you were arranging to take his body to Agrigento. To the Maggiore family plot."

"It was what he wanted, dear."

"Yes, Agrigento is where he wished to be buried. Auntie Nan and my mother have already left for Sicily. Auntie Nan is a Maggiore, and knows how things are . . . taken care of in Agrigento. As does my mother."

"Of course, dear. Of course they do. It is, of course, a very sad occasion, but it will, of course, be good to have them there. I welcome their help."

"Of course you do. And my mother, Auntie Nan. My mother and all the Sicilian relatives will be waiting for you."

A LEGAL VIGILENT

"Eddie Feinblatt is now Mareike's lawyer."

"What? That's not possible, Eddie is . . ."

"I know, Auntie Nan. No time to discuss that now. Get the first plane to Italy. Go to the family in Agrigento as fast as you can. And don't answer your phone. I've told Mareike that you and Mammina were already in Italy waiting for Pappino's body. Mareike plans to take Papp's body to Agrigento."

"The family will throw her over the cliff!"

"The family can do what it thinks best. But enough wishful thinking. I need to move. Right now, I'm sitting like an idiot on the floor of a toilet-stall, talking to you on my mobile phone, while watching for black sling-back shoes or silver and black cowboy boots."

"You're what?"

"Never mind. I've got to ring off now. Just go. You and Mammina need to be in Sicily. I will accompany Pappino's body and meet you there, once all the arrangements here are made. And could you ring cousin Giuseppino in Agrigento before you leave, and give him all the information?"

"Sure. I'll call him from the Montréal airport, so I can leave the apartment quicker. This line shouldn't be busy, in case the Dutchies phone here. You're a good girl, Ellissina. I'll take the first flight they give me."

"Perfect. And please call Mammina. Explain the situation and ask her to meet you in Agrigento. She just got back to Vancouver. I hate asking her to get on another plane so fast, but I know she'll want to be there."

"You must want to kill that Mareekie!"

"Not an option. Please, just hurry . . . oops, I see shoes. Gotta go."

Rang off, scooted onto toilet seat, flushed unused toilet. Opened door.

Mareike was studying her face, blotting reapplied fire-engine red lipstick to her labial sausages. She spoke into the mirror. "Just freshening up a bit, dear . . . Ellissa, I've been thinking . . . there really isn't any reason for me to go to Sicily. I mean, Johnny's burial wishes have been known for years . . . And with his family all there, I feel . . . I would be . . . intruding. I'll just be in the way . . ."

"Oh, I'm sure the Maggiores, and my mother, would . . . make a place for you . . . where you would not be in the way."

She opened her eyes beyond even their permanent surgical stare. Good, Mareike, I thought, staring back. You've got it in one. You don't want to be anywhere near Pappino's people. Or my mother. Or me.

"But . . . someone needs to accompany the body."

"I can do that, Mareike. In Canadian law, you have to ship a body via a licensed funeral home. The process of getting my father from the funeral home to the airline and then to Sicily will take a few days. It starts with moving the person from hospital to funeral parlour. We have one. Auntie Nan made those arrangements for my father when he had his first heart problems. Just in case. With his written consent. I also have London permission from him, had he died in England. There are post-mortem forms to sign . . ."

"Well, I am his legal wife, now his legal widow . . ."

"And I'm his first-born daughter. His legal . . . vigilant. Mareike, there is nothing for you in these forms. This is not about his money. Nor about his real estate holdings. This is about his body. His body is not worth very much money. Perhaps you'd get something for the parts . . ."

"Ellissa, please! You're just upset . . ."

"Yes. My father is dead and I'm upset. How extraordinary. Look, I'll accompany Pappino to Agrigento. I would've gone in any case. I can speak the local dialect. I want to be with his family, with my family, with my mother. I'll ring the appropriate airlines, and then ring Agrigento today, to tell them when Pappino and I will be arriving . . ."

My eyes filled. Water rolled down my cheeks. I wiped it away abruptly, then bit down on my finger, as all the Maggiores did to keep from sobbing or screaming. Mareike moved closer, making some sort of sympathy face. Don't touch me, I thought. You, of all people, must not touch me now.

With her usual sensitivity, and recognising grief as a centuries-old cue for an embrace, Mareike hugged me to her. I did the only thing possible. Threw up on her black silk suit.

MAJOR AND DAUGHTERS,
DI MARCO AND SONS

I collected the post-mortem hospital documents. The woman guiding me through this asked about the two Ellissa Majors.

"Yes. I gather that Petra Major, my half-sister, said she was me."

"She did more than that. She had cards with your name on them. We, naturally, asked for proof of her identity. She had England cards – library, pharmacy . . . and a driver's licence. She also knew your middle name."

I knew about "Giovanna." Did not know about the English I.D.

The flyer for the group show at "Rubin and Hall Galleries – New York, Berlin, Paris, Tokyo" was still on my hotel writing desk. I rang the gallery. A heavily accented voice answered: "Gud aiftuhnoon. Roobin an' Hawl Galleries. How may I help yew?"

"May I speak with Petra Major. She's an artist in your show."

"Yes. Mizz Maydguh isn't heea at the momentt. She's at where she's staying. Are you a vizhuwul awts journalistt?"

"No, I'm a family member. She left a number with me. 212-534-90 . . ."

"Yes. That's the correct numbuh. You should cawl huh theuh."

Before cawling Petra, I rang Di Marco and Sons Funeral Home.

It would be unseemly for a funeral director to be overly jolly and jovial. That said, Mrs. Adelina Di Marco had perhaps the saddest face

I'd ever seen. A tiny apple-doll face cross-hatched by many thread-fine lines, the sort of lines usually found inside the palm of a hand. Softly clacking teeth rested uneasily inside puffy cheeks. Her mouth was thin-lipped and downturned, book-ended by deep, equally down-turned marionette folds. Inside this face, above a narrow beaky nose, were two shiny, darkest-brown eyes, below drooping, slightly triangu-lated upper lids. Covered in black from head to foot (except for a gold wedding band on her left hand), she looked like a Halloween costume renter who'd forgotten the pointy hat.

I followed her into an office; a room with oak and burgundy leather furniture made to accommodate a larger person.

"When Vic, my late husband, God rest his soul, died, three years ago, I took over the business. Beh, it's a lot of work, but I worked by Vic's side for thirty-seven years. And the kids help me."

"Your sons?"

"Daughters. We only had daughters. Vic, my late husband, God rest his soul, thought "'V. Di Marco and Daughters' looked wrong. He said Italians don't want dead bodies handled by girls. My daughter Assunta is actually the licensed funeral director here. But Vic wanted 'and Sons.' Assunta doesn't mind. She told me that, when she meets somebody at a party or someplace, she says she's an anthropologist, which is her other degree. It means she studies people. Which it's true she does. Here also, she studies people. She says she doesn't have to tell guys that some of the people she studies are dead . . . Would you like some coffee or tea, Missus Major? Something to eat? A sandwich? We have lovely biscotti, and I can order you a sandwich. Please, have a seat."

I sat, in a leather armchair across from her enormous oak and leather desk. She sat behind the desk, almost disappearing under it, despite a black velvet pillow on her straight-backed oak chair. "I'm *Doctor* Major, the deceased's daughter. Thank you, I'm not hungry at the moment, but coffee – milk, no sugar – would be lovely."

"Certainly." She pressed a button on her large black phone.

"Assunta. Please ask Tina to bring a coffee with milk, no sugar. And some biscotti. Thank you . . . It's important, Doctor Major, to eat in times of grief. Eating is always important, but in times of grief it is very important. My late husband, God rest his soul, ate maybe too much, but . . ."

An hour later, I brought the funeral parlour papers to the woman at the hospital, and, from her office, rang Air Canada.

The Dead Body Rules (the Air Canada woman didn't call them that, but that's what they were) required three days on ice (she didn't say "on ice" either) before the body could fly. During this time, I needed to secure what was called "a Mortuary Passport" for Pappino, as well as proof of his birth in Agrigento. I did this, and left both items with Mrs. Di Marco, who informed me that, body and coffin, at $10.64 a kilo, it would cost $2,660 to ship Papp to Rome, plus about $400 on top of that from Rome to Palermo. I put all costs on my credit card, as neither the hospital nor the funeral home could accept English cheques, and my Montréal account contained only what Pappino called "walking-around money."

Mrs. Di Marco gave me a receipt and a large manila envelope containing all the documents. I would be expected to show these to airline and customs officials at each stage of the journey. Except the mortuary passport. That would rest on my father's chest inside the coffin, which would remain sealed from "point of origin" to "final destination." While travelling, there would be a small plastic window ("Strong plastic," said Mrs. D, "bulletproof") in the top of the coffin, through which Pappino and passport could be viewed by consular officers, airport officials and by me. Once we reached Agrigento, the coffin could be unsealed and the plastic window replaced by wood. "They have to be sure," she said, "that they have the same guy, the same deceased person all the way through to final destination."

"All the way through to final destination. Same guy," I repeated, nodding, wondering how many dead people might otherwise be involved in going from point of origin to a final destination One per stop? Possibly. You could get rid of a lot of dodgy dead bodies that way, were it not for seal, plastic window and mortuary passport.

Air Canada flew to Rome. I would then take an Alitalia flight to Palermo, Sicily. There were no commercial flights from Palermo to Agrigento, so I'd have to make "small craft arrangements" – twelve-seater plane, helicopter or ground transport. I agreed and rang off.

There were three identical sets of documents – insurance, responsibilities, rights of accompanying relative(s), rights of non-accompanying immediate family, rights of airline, etc; one set for me, one for Air Canada and Alitalia, another for Di Marco and Sons.

Auntie Nan had signed each set. As the "party accompanying the body and its housing" I co-signed. Then, with death covering me like fine silt, returned to my hotel, bathed, and slept.

I dreamt Pappino and I were dancing, both of us adults, in Maidenhead-on-Thames – the room in which, years earlier he'd married Jennifer. In the dream, he was marrying Jennifer again, as if for the first time, and, in the wonkiness of dreamtime, a boy Davy, who'd not yet been born in the actual J & J wedding period, watched us from behind a potted palm. Mrs. Di Marco screeched from outside a large, glassless window, flapping her black crow arms, saying "Beh, beh, God rest his soul!" In reverse of the years-earlier wedding, Papp had the toes of his black-stockinged dead feet over the tops of my shoes. His dead eyes were closed. His face was grey and yellow. He smelled of *Acqua di Parma* cologne, as he had in life, and, ever so slightly, of putrefaction. We waltzed. People moved away from us, pressed themselves against the rounded walls. Perhaps to give us room, as the dancing guests of honour. Perhaps due to the stench of a decaying body.

When I awoke, I realised that the dream-invading stench was from a room-service egg-salad sandwich that was growing a culture in my room. I put the tray of rotting sandwich in the hall, then dressed and ricocheted around downtown Montréal for a while, drinking coffee and looking in windows. Stopped in Notre Dame Cathedral and quietly cried. What in hell, I thought, was I to do with my numb and soggy self while waiting to fly my father to his homeland? Coming out of the cathedral, I almost stumbled over a dead pigeon. Went back to the hotel and booked a flight to New York. Before leaving for the airport, I rang Petra's New York number.

"Hi. Roberta Rubin here. And not here. Or not able to take your call at this time. You can try me at the gallery or leave a message after the beep. Until March first, messages may also be left for Petra Major, who is part of our wonderful new show at the Rubin-Hall Gallery. Peace."

I chose not to leave a message.

New York:
Acts of Violence
in Life and Art

In late January of 2002, the people of New York were still very much on terror alert, and nowhere more than in Scary-Airy places. John F. Kennedy Airport, named for an assassinated president, was the largest Scary-Airy place in New York. And, to my outsider's eyes, maggoty fear wriggled everywhere. Before boarding in Montréal, I'd had to surrender the Swiss Army knife Pappino had given me for my thirteenth birthday. At Kennedy Airport, I retrieved it, now thickly wrapped in heavy black electrical tape. The woman behind the retrieval desk put the taped knife in a heavy plastic bag, which in turn was taped.

Knife acceptably slowed to neutral, my carry-on wheely-bag was inspected, as it had been in Montréal. There was an unusually long queue for this inspection.

"Sorry about this, Missus . . . Major. We don't usually inspect previously inspected carry-on during arrivals. We're on an orange."

"On an orange?" I envisioned a seal balanced on a beachball.

. "Orange alert."

"What is an orange alert?"

"One before red." She looked at my passport. "Don't you have those in England?"

"They didn't when I left. They may now. We have a large – No, Ellissa. Do not say "Muslim." If you say Muslim, you will be here for hours – population of people flying out of England. And, of course, into England as well." I smiled. She smiled. "Of course." She returned my passport and pointed to an endless-looking queued mass of humanity. "Those are the Alien lines. All non-resident aliens must clear through there."

Given the extensive snaking of the "Alien" queues, a quick pee seemed prudent. I went to the women's loo, with its funny line drawing of a woman (I'd often wondered if aliens from other planets expect to meet tiny people in A-line dresses; eyeless, faceless, with thin rectangular legs. Perhaps they do meet them. Perhaps these loo-drawing people hide from earthlings, revealing themselves only to Martians, Venusians, and others highly enough evolved to interact with them).

I joined the Aliens, behind a Sikh family. I knew that many Americans (and many others outside South Asia) could not tell one turban from another and were tending to treat all turban-wearers with a combination of paranoia and casual racism. When the inspectors got to me, my interrogation would follow the Sikh's longer one. In 2002 New York, I thought, this turban-related caution did not make much sense – those with mayhem in mind tended to avoid what would be seen as "ethnic dress."

An hour later, I watched as a grey-haired woman with a Scots burr had her large knitting bag checked for bombs. ("It's an Afghan. I'm making it for my new grandson.") They took her into a little side room. Perhaps it was the word Afghan.

Then it was my turn.

"Ellissa Major? Missus?"

"Doctor."

"And what is the purpose of your visit to New York, Doctor Major?"

"I'm going to an art show. My half-sister is an artist. Her work is in a gallery show here."

"Oh. Does she live in New York?"

"No. She lives in the Netherlands. She came to New York for this show."

"I see. And you are a British national?"

"Yes."

"You live in South . . . world?"

"Wold. Southwold."

"And that's in Suffolk? Is that near London?"

"Not far. It's in the countryside, about three hours by train from London. Or a bit longer, given the current state of train travel."

"Is there a problem with the trains in England?"

(Oh damn, I thought, this man is not going to be interested in what Mrs. Thatcher did to British Rail.) "Not really. Some of them need to be modernised is all." I smiled. He smiled back.

"And you're . . . a 'small animal veterinarian?' How small?"

"I'm not small. The animals are small."

"Yeah, that's what I meant. How small are the animals."

I giggled. The inspector did not. It was, therefore, a very short giggle. "It just means dogs and cats mostly. Sometimes reptiles, hamsters, birds . . ."

"Have you handled birds recently?"

"Not for at least a year. I have papers from Ste. Bernadette Hospital in Montréal. They checked me out for that very reason when I came to Montréal to see my father. He was in hospital there."

"Was? Where is he now?"

"At Di Marco's Funeral Parlour. He has . . . passed away. I'm going to fly with his body in two days."

"To London."

"No, to Sicily." I wished I'd said Italy. Too many people think Sicilians are mobsters. I'd sometimes thought this myself, but only about my parents.

"Your father is Sicilian?"

"Yes, originally."

"Brava! So am I. Fracci, Damiano Fracci."

"Maggiore. Ellissa Maggiore. My grandfather changed the name. To help with employment in Canada. My father was born Giovanni Paolo Maggiore."

"My brother did the name thing. He's 'Forrest.' I kept 'Fracci.'"

"'Major' was easier in England."

"Yeah. My brother thinks 'Forrest' is easier. Me, I'm good with Fracci. *Molto piacere.* Pleased to meet you."

"*Anch' io,*" I replied. This was another thing about Sicilians: In Sicily, people from the next town are *stranieri* – strangers, but in the wider world we are all family, all of us against anybody else, anywhere. Damiano Fracci and I shook hands, him taking one of mine in two of his. He said he was sorry about my father's passing. He said God should rest my father's soul. He said he hoped I'd enjoy my sister's art show. My interview was over. Me, my wheely-bag and my taped Swiss Army knife were free in New York.

I took a taxi to the Lyndhurst, a pleasant but inexpensive little hotel in Manhattan's Greenwich Village district. I'd stayed there twice before, years earlier, on trips to New York with Nick Brown. He was attending conferences there. I was his girlfriend. We were in love.

In my room, I wrapped myself in the robe provided by the hotel and headed down the corridor to shower. Shower and toilet in the corridor was what made the clean, well-situated Lyndhurst far less pricey than other similar hotels in New York. Apparently, many Americans felt squeamish about sharing the loo. The hotel was always filled with Europeans, Asians, Africans and younger Yanks, who were used to living in dorms with shared "facilities."

Back in my room, I dressed in black tights, white polo-necked close-fitting shirt and a black trousers-suit. Eyes lined and mascara-ed, lips coloured and glossed, short hair fashionably rumpled and gelled, I headed off, flyer in hand, to the Rubin and Hall Gallery.

Children's plush toy animals, of pink or blue synthetic fur, floated in outsized glass jars filled with clear and coloured liquid. Dolls' heads and arms hung from the ceiling. A very long necklace of chicken beaks and feet, interspersed with bright red Mareike-like plastic lips was strung in scooped half-circles across the length of one white wall.

In an L-shaped corner of the large loft space, I came to Petra's work.

It was the piece from the flyer: a wren's face and wing forcing their way out of a second-storey lace-curtained doll's house window. Two toy fire engines howled at low volume outside the four-columned porch of the posh-looking white house, their tiny red roof lights spinning round and round, while a red-orange flame effect flickered against the house's exterior. I bent to look into the windows. The tiny rooms were filled with doll furniture, but the only animal life was the taxidermically preserved brown bird struggling to escape.

"Ellissa! You came! I didn't expect you to. And you look . . . all glossy and glam. We're even dressed as sisters." It was sort of true. Petra and I wore black wide-legged trousers-suits with white stretchy shirts underneath. I looked at the other gallery-goers. "Well Petra, I seem to be dressed as a sister to most of the women here . . . and a number of the men."

"Art gallery uniform, I suppose. What do you think of 'Bird/House?'"

"It's good. Clear and powerful. Imaginative. I like it."

"Truly?"

"Truly."

An ample and very tall woman, floppy-choppy hair of many colours, including red, blue and green, walked towards us, bearing two glasses of bubbly pale golden wine. She too wore a black trousers-suit, its mid-thigh-length jacket loosely fitted over a shimmery silver boat-necked top. She grinned, revealing large white teeth with a gap between the two front uppers. Her voice was as throaty as Petra's, but far louder, perhaps to be heard properly over the din of the room. The accent was that half-Brit/half-Yank mix frequently favoured by actors.

"Hullo Ellissa. I'm Roberta Rubin. Please, have a glass of champagne. You too, Pet."

"Thanks. This is your gallery then?"

"Yes. My long-time partner, Renée Hall, died last year. We were partners in life and art."

"Renée brought me into the gallery," Petra said with some pride. "She saw my show in Amsterdam five years ago."

Roberta flung an arm over Petra's thin shoulders. Her size made the tiny Petra look like an androgynous child. "We both loved Pet's work. And the New York critics seem to agree. Octavian Lester, our most important art critic, says her work has 'urgency' and 'imagination,' and is 'a standout.'"

"He also said 'haunted and haunting.' I liked that, 'haunted and haunting.' Petra grinned and then her voice softened almost to a whisper. "I really am surprised that you actually came, Ellissa. Sur-prised and glad."

"I'm also glad I came, Petra. But I don't want to crowd your opening night . . ."

"Oh, you're not. I'm so pleased that . . ."

"I do have to speak with you though. Some family business. Nothing worrying. You've been left some money . . ."

Her eyes brightened. "Really? That's great!"

"I'm only here for one more day. Might we meet for late breakfast or lunch tomorrow?"

"Absolutely. There's a good coffee and breakfast place just on this corner. Vinny's Garage."

"A restaurant in a garage?"

Both women laughed. "No, no. It had once been a garage. Roberta says the two ultra chic gay guys who turned it into a restaurant kept the name because Joey, one of them, thinks it's 'ironically butch,' whatever that means. Let's meet at noon. You can get either breakfast or lunch at that time."

"Great. Vinny's at noon. And here's to 'haunted and haunting.'"

Major Rules About Lying

Boys and girls are told, in both secular and religious settings, that lying is bad, that it is punishable by both God and man, and that we're not supposed to do it. Ever. We are also told this at home. Some of us are.

When I was nine, Geoff Dale, a Peter Rabbit schoolmate (and someone I sort of fancied, in the vague prismatic way nine-year-olds do; merging fairy tales with things about hair, eyes, smiles), told me he'd found buried treasure in Highgate Cemetery. He invited me to see this treasure, and said he would give me "a gold doubloon." I'd no idea what a doubloon was. Geoff said they were "twice the size of sin-gloons, and very shiny." This great heap of treasure sounded wonderful and certainly worth seeing. Honoured at being chosen ("You're the only person I've told, Ellissa. You must swear not to tell anyone else."), I swore, and off we went.

There was no buried treasure at Highgate Cemetery. There was only Geoff, wanting to show me his, wanting to see mine. My crush instantly disappeared and I was furious. Mine was mine and none of his business, and his was something I truly did not want to see, except perhaps by accident when he didn't know I was looking. Most importantly, he had lied. He had done that thing we were never supposed to do. Or so I had been told.

Until I asked my father whether people were allowed to lie (without telling him what happened at Highgate, as I was certain that Papp, in dramatic and embarrassingly public fashion, would seek and smite Geoff).

"Has someone lied to you?"

"No."

He was in his newspaper-reading chair and looked up at me, standing in the archway, in black knee-socked feet and school uniform. He smiled. "Come in."

"I don't want to disturb your reading. I just wondered if . . ."

"Please, Ellissina. There's no reason for us to shout across the room at each other." (We weren't shouting.) "I'm always glad to see you. Come."

I sat in my child-sized wine-red leather chair, which exactly matched his grown-up's wine-red leather chair, crossing my legs at the ankles as I'd been taught to do in Deportment class. Papp was still smiling, His eyes looked friendly. He put his large hand, the one with his university football ring, on my knee, and spoke softly. "You just lied to me. When I asked if anyone had lied to you, you said no. Who lied to you?"

I felt my face flush, and stared at my feet. Involuntarily, I giggled. "Just . . . somebody at school. Not anything big. But definitely a lie."

"Ah. That's OK. If it isn't a serious lie, or a scary lie, you don't have to tell me the details. It's your business. You have a right to have private things. Unless you're in trouble, or in danger. Trouble or danger, you should tell me. Deal?"

"Deal. No trouble, no danger. I just wondered . . . because, at school, people tell these little lies a lot, and Grownups all say we're not supposed to do that – to lie."

"Right. People do tell little lies. We all do. I do. You do – and you will again. Me too. What you need to know is when it's OK to lie, and when it isn't." He drew on his pipe. I liked the smell. Sometimes, somewhere outside our flat, I'd smell that smell and think "someone is smoking Papp's tobacco" – as if that particular tobacco belonged to my father, and that, somehow, these other people had got hold of some.

After a few moments, his "considering something" face relaxed and he looked into my eyes. "I understand why they're strict about it in school, and in church – nobody wants to raise lots of little liars. In the bigger world though, the one you live in outside of school and church, the one you'll grow up to live in, there aren't always hard and fast rules about lying. The rules can . . . sort of shift with the situation. Especially with emergencies, when you think you're in some kind of danger . . ."

"Danger? What sort of danger?"

"Don't be frightened. Danger isn't the important part of my answer to your question . . ."

"Like what, though? What sort of danger?"

He laughed. "Come here. Sit on my lap. Put your head on my chest."

We both knew I was almost too big for lap-sitting. And both knew that I still liked to do it. I climbed onto his lap, swung my legs over to the side of his left leg (careful not to kick him in his "man parts," which I'd done once, by accident, and knew I shouldn't do again, because it hurt). I rested my cheek against his chest, closing my eyes and breathing in the pipe smell. "There. Feel safer?"

I nodded my head against his chest, my cheek feeling the curly hairs under his pale blue and white striped shirt.

"Good. Anyway, we can tell lies for three reasons. We can lie when we are protecting someone from fear – 'You'll be fine, it will be all right,' we say. You're not sure things will be all right, but you want to calm someone. Calm can reduce fear. Or we lie when we don't want to hurt someone's feelings. We say 'that dress is a pretty colour,' instead of 'that dress is too tight,' or 'I like your hair that way,' rather than 'I hated your hair the other way.' And we – you – can also lie when it might save your life. Make sense?"

"I'm not sure."

"Let's review. Tell me the three times when it's okay to lie."

"Uh . . . one, to protect someone or calm them down. Two, to not hurt someone's feelings. Three, to save your life."

"You've got it. Oh, there is one other time when you might have to lie. When you need to get someone to do something for you. Something important. You give them a reason, a lie-reason, because if you give them the true reason, they won't do what you need them to do. Then, once they do what you needed to have them do, if you like them, you should tell them the truth . . . and you can also tell them why you told the lie. Make sense now?"

I sat up and looked into the family eyes. "Sort of . . . I need to think about it for a bit."

He rubbed his index finger against my cheek. "Yes, you think about it. And if you have more questions I'll try to answer them. Tricky stuff, lying and truth."

Tricky stuff, indeed. Over the years, I'd tried to apply Pappino's rules about when to lie.

I had lied to Petra, saying the magic word (money). I thought this word would bring her to me. It did.

BANISHER'S DAUGHTER
AND HER SISTER

"*Hooder morhen*. Excuse my Dutch. It is harder for me to think in English before coffee. You already have your coffee. I will get mine."

I watched her walk to the counter. Faded jeans, white running shoes and the pale pink quilted bomber jacket she had worn in Montréal. Her tiny buttocks like two hard round melons, thighs wider than arms but narrower than legs, spiked, and gelled yellow hair bouncing as she walked.

She returned with a white mug of latte, and sat across from me. "Booth, yah? I remembered from Montréal that you like booths. I thought of this when I suggested Vinny's." She laughed, ducking her head slightly, the way dogs do when they are the canine equivalent of embarrassed. "It is also near to where I am staying, so I would not be late to meet you. After all the champagne and not so much sleep. And we look like clothing sisters again, blue jeans both."

"Petra. I know about the library card and the driver's licence."

She looked at me; unflinching, almost neutral, her lower lip jutting forward slightly. The way mine did when I was going to stand my ground. The way our father's would, for the same reason. "Who told you? The woman from the hospital?"

"Yes."

"Yah. I thought that could happen. I told Mama it could happen. She said it didn't matter."

"In Montréal, you said you wanted nothing to do with your mother. That was a lie."

"No, it's true. My mother is a selfish and greedy old woman. A pimp of her daughters. My life is better without her."

"A pimp? You mean . . ."

"She sold me to men, rich old men she knew, for money. Me and Floris. After Daddy cut us off."

"Did our father know you were being . . . sold? Did you tell him?"

"Of course not. If I told him he would just think I was a worse pig than he already thought. One of the whore daughters of whore mother. He did not know that I thought Mama was an even bigger whore than he thought."

"If you thought this, why did you help kill him?"

"Money. Mama telephoned. I picked up the phone – I almost never do this with her. She said when Papa died she would get all his money. We signed a contract for my share. She said a mother and daughter didn't need a contract. Isn't that crazy, Ellissa? That she would say this to someone who actually knew her. Goddamn! She thinks the whole world is stupid! I have a good contract. From a big lawyer in The Hague. I'll probably have to take her to court in the end, but . . ."

"The I.D., the library card, the Dutch driving licence in my name . . . ?"

"A forger. All artists know forgers. People who forge Michelangelo and Van Gogh can easily forge a little driving licence. Mama gave me her 'wife' paper, all signed and said I would need identifications to release Daddy from hospital. She said you or Davy must also sign to take Daddy out. She told me she tried to pull out his life wires but the doctor caught her. She told him she was just making Daddy more comfortable. She thinks the doctor knew she was lying but he could not prove nothing. She said also . . . the thing you told me in Montréal. That Daddy didn't realise he was old, and that when he saw all the old people it would make him die faster. I did not think it would be . . . so very fast."

I don't know if Petra's voice had actually turned metallic, or if I was having some sort of panic-driven tonal distortion. "In Montréal, you said you were sorry he died. Were you?"

"No. He was a shit. He, for years, broke all my heart bones. I did not want to hurt you, Ellissa. In Montréal, you seemed like a nice person. I . . . liked being with you." She smiled for a second – the smile of an approval-seeking child. Then her face tightened, lower lip pushing forward. "If he did not care that I was alive or dead, then I did not care if he was alive or dead. If he saw me, if he said 'Hello, my daughter,' if he reached out a hand to me, I would have said to hell with Mama. To hell with the money. But he did none of that. Nothing. So I wanted him to die. And wanted him to know it was me who caused it. I wore pale pink clothing because he had liked me best in that colour. He would buy me always things in that colour. Floris got red things. I got pink. When he was spinning in his wheelchair, in that room full of old people, I knelt down and said, very quiet, 'Hello, Daddy. It's me. Petra. Your daughter Petra. I brought you here. Because you are old, and this is where you belong, old man.' I was looking into his eyes. He was looking back, but he did not know me. He just stared at me. No expression. I said again that I was his daughter Petra, and there was again no reaction. His eyes were alert, but he did not know me. I just wanted him to know me. If he knew me, if he offered any . . . family, I would have fought to save him. It was probably too late. He was so gaga."

I spoke softly, as I'd been trained to do at times such as these. "His eyes were, you say, 'alert.' I think he did know you. He always told me: 'When the bastards hurt you, don't show it. Don't let them see it on your face. Go cold.'" Petra's hands, on the faux-marble table, clenched into fists. "You're wrong. He did *not* know me. He was lost. He was . . ."

"No, Petra. He was fully aware, fully conscious. He just wasn't going to give you the satisfaction. You had him. He was helpless.

Except in this one way. He could still deny you the only thing you wanted – recognition."

She stood up, shiver-shaking like an Italian greyhound. "Fuck you! Fuck him! He was gaga! I know what I saw!"

"Have it your way, Petra. Do you have the cards? The false identity cards?"

Reaching into her black leather shoulder bag, she extracted a card case, riffled through it, and pulled out three cards. Dropping the case back into her bag, she threw the cards onto the table. "I still know the same forger. I can get more cards."

"I suppose you can. But you don't need them anymore. Johnny Major is dead. His will has disappeared. If you want his money, you should make new cards saying you're Mareike DeLyn. Given how much surgery Marunkle has had, you might be able to pass, in a dim light."

She laughed, quickly, almost soundlessly. "In a way, that's funny. I'm still glad you came to my show. It was . . . good to have a sister for a minute."

"You already have a sister. A twin."

"Floris is a stupid cow. She feeds at one end and shits at the other."

"So does everybody."

"Floris feeds more and shits more. I liked you better. I suppose that now it is impossible. For us to be sisters, I mean."

"We always will be sisters, Petra. I just don't want to see you again. Ever."

Her eyes popped. I believe she thought the shared laugh had something to do with our future. It did not. It meant nothing. Not after what she'd done.

"A banisher. You're a banisher. Like him."

"Yes. I'm very like him."

"When Daddy went, when he completely left, after seeming to love me so much, do you know what Mama said? When I could not stop weeping and calling for him? She said, 'Oh Petra, nothing stays.' You can see that in two ways – one is that everything, everyone goes away – but also that nothing is what stays. Nothing, emptiness, staying, always."

She sniffed sharply and snap-turned her face away, thrusting her hands into her jeans. Then, turning back, she looked down and into my eyes, her own eyes cold and neutral; the flat stare I'd seen in Montréal. "What about the money? You said there was money for me . . ."

"There isn't any money for you that I know about."

"Then why did you say . . . ?"

"To get you to come here."

She sighed. Her eyes were shiny. "It worked."

"Yes."

"I would have come anyway. To see you."

"I couldn't be sure of that."

"Ellissa?"

"Yes?"

"If you see me, I mean accidentally, somewhere in the world, will you say hello?

"Probably."

She smiled. I didn't. "Well. Goodbye then . . . my sister."

"Goodbye, Petra."

An Old Club Fighter

I stared at the forged cards. Library, London; Driver's Licence, Amsterdam (with her photo); Boots Chemists, London. I scooped them up and bunged them into my handbag. My body felt heavy, bruised. The body of an old club fighter who was still standing, waiting to be declared the winner, to be free to drop to the ground. I was not ready to move, so sat for a while in Vinny's butch garage, drinking coffee, listening to Vivaldi.

A small balletic girl with a long neck and a lateral lisp asked if I'd be staying for lunch. I said no, thanked her, paid the bill and walked out into a clear, crisp winter day.

I tightened my grey scarf and pulled the black toque over my ears. Without knowing why, I began to walk downtown, the opposite direction to that of my hotel. After two blocks of walking, I understood the choice. I was heading towards the World Trade Center.

Closer to the site, there was a strange smell. It was faint at first, growing stronger as I continued south. I knew this smell, but could not place it. Its name stood just outside the section of my brain where words are kept. Then I got it. It was a smell from when I had long hair and still smoked. In passionate debate, hands flying about, the lit cigarette between my fingers would connect briefly with my hair. Burning hair. Burnt hair. It seemed to my nose that all of lower Manhattan reeked of burnt hair. I turned and headed north to my hotel, away from the smell.

There were three messages awaiting me. All said the same thing: Call your brother.

"At last! I knew you were in New York. I knew you were at the Lyndhurst. I knew buggerall else. So I rang the Lyndhurst. Where are you?"

"Now, I am at the Lyndhurst. I'm so sorry, Davy. A lot has happened. It will all keep until I see you. Sorry I've been incommunicado."

"When are you coming back?"

"Soon. I have to take Papp's body to Agrigento and be there for the funeral. They're Sicilians; it could take a week or two."

"Do Papp's people know that I would be there as well, if I weren't shooting this telly thing?"

"I'll tell them. They'll understand. Anyway, I'll fly to London immediately after the funeral. We'll catch up on info and then I'll go back to Southwold. Bet has been managing the clinic on her own for too long. She's almost a pensioner but she works harder than most twenty-two-year olds. And says she wants to stay on with me for as long as I want it. Which is forever."

"Forever. I've been thinking about forever. About Papp. About us. About how children believe in forever."

"Me too. And about what can happen when forever ends. So much has happened in this . . . this 'post-forever' period. It's been like . . ."

"Being dragged, very slowly, face-down, over pavement, by horses?"

I laughed. "Well, I was going for something less theatrical, but that'll do. Love you. Miss you."

"Me too you."

COLLECTING PAPPINO

Leaving Airport America was as fraught as entering it. A blond child of about five had to take off his shoes, which were checked for explosives. I was asked to remove my Victorian starburst brooch, as its very dull starpoints "could be used as a weapon." And again I surrendered my heavily taped Swiss Army knife, which would be returned to me in Montréal.

I then went from Dorval airport to Di Marco's to authorise Papp's coffin being transferred to Air Canada's "cold room," and to make sure he was in it. He was. Great hair. Strong face. Too much makeup. It helped that he looked masked. Made it easier to look without crying, without screaming. Mrs. Di Marco assured me that he was properly done up for travel, and would get to Agrigento without starting to smell ("Your father, God rest his soul, is good for about a week. After a week, beh, you should bury him").

With Papp's coffin in the freezing undercarriage of a plane, and all documents presented to and reviewed by the appropriate authorities, I telephoned Cousin Giuseppino in Sicily, saying we were on our way. Then I asked to speak with Auntie Nan.

"Ellissina? That you?" she rasped.

"Yes. I've got the documents, and, thus far, all is well. I'm at the Montréal airport. I fly to Rome with Pappino's . . . with Pappino, in an hour. Then Rome to Palermo. In Palermo, I'll arrange for a small plane or a train to . . ."

"Wait, Ellissina. Pino set up something about that . . . Giuseppino!"

After a flurry of Sicilian dialect, Auntie Nan said, "Ellissa? There'll be a big black car at Palermo airport. The driver is Liddru. He was a kid with your father and me. Good guy. He'll have a sign saying *'Signora Maggiore.'* Would you rather it says *'Dottore?'* And 'Major?'"

Thinking in two languages simultaneously, I was startled to note that the Italian *Dottore* sounded so much like the English "daughter." And knew that asking for *Dottore*, so that I could hear 'daughter,' would only be seen by the Sicilians as an *Inglese* showing-off.

"*Signora Maggiore*" is fine. Please give him my flight number. 334. It's due in Palermo at three-twenty in the afternoon – fifteen hundred hours and twenty minutes."

"*Va bene. Buon viaggio*, Ellissina. Have a safe journey." She rang off.

I was surprised to realise that I'd not asked if my mother were there.

ROME:
THE IMPOSSIBLE APPEARS

"Attenzione! Attenzione, prego! Il passeggero Nicholson Brown del volo Alitalia due venti tré é, pregato recarsi al telefono bianco del bancone Alitalia al' terminal uno. Grazie. Your attention please. Would arriving passenger Nicholson Brown, Mister Brown, of Alitalia flight two-twenty three, Mister Nicholson Brown, please come to the white courtesy telephone at the counter of Alitalia Airlines in terminal one? Thank you."

There are unlikely things. There are improbable things. This thing, however, was impossible. I went to the Alitalia counter and stood next to the white telephone, waiting for the impossible to appear. He did.

"Hello, Nick."

It had never been easy to surprise Nicholson Brown. He's one of those lazy-smiling laid-back American southerners who seem always to have "evvythang under control." I noted with some pride and pleasure that he was totally gobsmacked. He looked at me as if I were an apparition. Then he smiled, mostly because the smile was his version of Papp's hand-through-hair gesture – it always bought him time.

"My Lord, Elly. It was you pagin' me?"

"No. But I heard the page . . . and it seemed I should at least say hello."

"Yes. Of course you should. I mean I'm glad you did. I'm delighted . . . but I'd better find out who did page me. Can you wait for me, while I do that?"

"Mm hm."

He turned the smile on the woman behind the counter. "Hello there. I'm Nicholson Brown. You paged me."

"Ah, *Signor* Brown. Yes, someone is telephoning to you. Just pick up this telephone, thank you."

"Hello, Nick Brown speaking. Hey, Annie. What's up? She put what through her lip? Oh Lord. When? Uh huh. Yeah, I bet. Did you take her to . . . ?"

Recognising a private domestic conversation, I moved farther from the courtesy telephone. The chatter continued for a while, concluding with "Me too. See you home. 'Bye."

Him too? Him too what? I love you? I love you too? See you home? Wife? Mother of girl-child who put . . . something through her lip?

Conversation concluded and Alitalia woman thanked, Nick turned his smile and big grey eyes on me. "Well now. Look at you. You look great, Elly . . . exactly the same."

"That's not possible, Nick. Not after fifteen years and an overnight flight. But it's a sweet thought."

"No, I mean it. The long hair is gone, and you've got these l'il grey guys here . . ." He lightly fluffed the wisps of silver at my temples. Damned if I didn't gasp. Quick small gasp, but a definite member of the gasp family. Lips parted. Eyes panicked. I felt these things happen. He saw them happen and took his hands away from the general area of my face.

"I'm no one to talk! Still gotta lotta hair, but In Louisville" (LOOuhville, he said, as he always had), they now call me The Silver Fox . . . which is what they call all the grey haired old guys, the ones who . . ."

". . . ain't too ugly."

He laughed. "You remember that?"

You remember that? The words I'd used with Petra about my middle name. She'd said she remembered everything about me. And I remembered everything about Ellissa Major and Nicholson Brown. Evvydamn thang.

"So, what are you doing in Rome?"

"International conference. Gerontology. You?

"Me too, gerontology. I'm here with my father."

"Oh. Is he well?"

"Not very. He's dead."

He moved to comfort me. Reflexively, I backed up. He stayed where he was. "I'm . . . so sorry, Elly. I know how much he . . ."

"It's all right, Nick. He was almost ninety. I'm accompanying his body to Sicily, to bury him in the village where he was born. It was his wish."

"Well . . . he certainly had a big life."

"Yes."

We stood there, looking into one another's eyes, wearing little closed-mouth smiles. "Well, I've got my suitcase, and nowhere to be until tomorrow morning. You have time for a drink? Here at the air-port?"

"Yes. My flight to Sicily goes tomorrow at noon. I have to book a room at the airport hotel."

"Before you do that, might we . . . find the bar, have a visit?"

"I'd like that. First, however, I must present my father's paperwork to the authorities and arrange for his safekeeping between flights . . ."

"Look, if it's too much . . ."

"No, Nick, it's not too much. 'Too much' has already happened. Having a drink with you is . . . something of an antidote for too much. Please, go to the bar. The one over there that says *Bravi*. I'll join you after I've done my documentary deeds. It shouldn't take long. I was the only person . . . in my situation on the flight from Montréal, and, with luck, that will hold true for Rome-Palermo. It's good you're here."

There have usually been men around me, though less so as I grow older (I'm not attracted to the young men who are attracted to me, and most men my age want women like the woman I was when younger; an independent alternative to the wife at home). There has been, however, only one man who could, sometimes all at once, make me laugh, make me think and make me want to be naked and skin-to-skin – and that man was, with no prior warning, sitting across from me in an Italian airport bar.

The following morning I would have to look into my father's coffin before the flight to make sure he'd not been removed and replaced with a public official, bags of heroin or a load of dirty socks. We'd then fly to Palermo, but before Palermo, before Agrigento, I was sitting under pink-bulb tracklights that almost effaced my fine facial lines and drinking gin and tonic at eight in the morning with Nick babybaby-baby Brown.

We laughed. We discussed George Bush and George Clooney. We got a room in the airport hotel.

Sometimes it's a dreadful mistake to make love, to have sex, to shag (never did know what to call that – just know it when it happens) with someone with whom you've not done that thing for a long while.

And sometimes it is a good idea.

If you're underslept, overstressed and having to bury the person dearest to you in all the world – it can be a good idea of symphonic benedictive proportions.

Nick, a doctor about to have sex with a woman he'd not seen in fifteen years, was gracious enough to unquestioningly (and with only a slight smile and raised eyebrow) accept the optimistic cluster of condoms I silently provided. In fact, Davy had provided them – a birthday gift shoved into my wheely-bag, "in case you fall in love or lust without warning." "Without warning" certainly applied to Nick Brown.

He was tall enough to pack extra weight inside suits. He'd got a love-handled waistline, slightly more barrelling in the chest. But the feel, the smell of him was a homecoming for the homeless – you knew you weren't from there, but you knew you were *of* there – and that there was of you.

After Nick's babybabybaby and the breathy giggling that almost always follows my orgasms, he held me. As ever, I wanted to suckle on his nipple, but remembered the old discussion: "I hate that, Elly. It gives me the heebie jeebies. It's like you haven't been weaned."

"I haven't. My mum wouldn't nurse me."

"Well, y're two for two, baby; I ain't gonna nurse you either."

We made love and slept and made love and slept. The second time we awakened it was dusk, with the sun setting behind the tangled AutoRoute.

"You good?" Nick asked, smiling at me.

"Yes, thanks. I'm very good indeed. And . . . how are you, sir?"

"Grand, madam, just grand. And I thank you for asking. A bit . . . funkier than I wanna be though. Let's have a shower."

Clean, wet-haired, both of us sprayed lightly with Nick's bloke-cologne (Davy's word for what makes him smell "butchy enough to not agitate the yobs, but clean and lovely as well"), we checked out the mini-bar, retrieving and opening a half-bottle of cold Pino Grigio.

Nick put on a terry robe, offering me the other one. I declined, tying a large towel around my lower body (as a long-time European beachgoer, I had no shyness about bare breasts. Lower body covering, however, was not about modesty – it was about Deportment – Mrs. Dearing always said that young ladies never sat with their legs apart. I was certain that flashing a post-coital furry naked vadge – unless you're doing what Davy calls "Bordello flirting" – was definitely not on for Ladies of any age).

"It's . . . good to see you, Nick."

He raised a water tumbler of yellow wine. "To . . . absent friends, suddenly present."

We toasted, drank, and then were suddenly self-conscious. Silence. Finally.

"May I ask about your now-life? You're married, yes?"

"Yes. 'Bout seven years."

"Congratulations. Kids?"

"A beautiful little girl. Five years old."

"That was the airport page?"

"Yeah. Lizzy, my daughter, was suckin' on the little wooden stick on one o' those tiny American flags, and she was runnin' at the same time. A splinter broke off into the inside of her cheek. Doctor got it out, but Lizzy was none too happy about the whole thing."

"Do you have a picture of her?" Always a dodgy moment. Does it defame your perfect daughter by showing her picture to the woman you've just shagged? Fatherly pride won that debate.

"Oh sure. Got three. Hang on, I'll get 'em." He was up and retrieving his wallet. "This is Miss Lizzy. This here's the bald baby. Good eyes though."

"Great eyes. Your eyes."

"That's what I think. Her mother's mouth and blonde hair, my eyes. And this is her kindergarten picture. Real serious. This one here's my favourite. Naked beautiful kid, havin' her bubble-bath, laughin' her head off."

"What made her laugh?"

"Her father. Her father's very funny, you know."

"Yes. I know."

We got quiet again, both thinking unfunny thoughts.

"More wine, Elly?"

"Yes, please."

I knew that opening the door to our dark room was going to be my job. I resented this; I wasn't the one who'd left without a word. Why did asking about it have to be my job? I knew why. Because I was "the girl" and guys rarely did unsolicited explanations. Not once in fifteen years did Nick do such a thing. Hell, he didn't even do solicited explanations. Not when he left, perhaps not ever. The Major/Maggiore family motto was Take Your Shot. I did.

"Nick, when you left, in the way-back-when, wasn't I worth an explanation? A letter? Something?"

He sighed. His eyes were soft. "Oh Elly. We're . . . so good here. You sure you want to do this now?"

"I don't know if we'll have another chance."

"Yeah, there's that." He sighed and got out of bed, walked to the window, turned to me.

"Elly. Before I left 'without a word' as you say, I had proposed to you. Asked you to be my wife. You do remember that part?"

I put on the available terry robe, not wishing to be the warrior without a uniform. My back to him, I said. "Please Nick, no sarcasm. I don't want to fight you." I faced him. "This matters to me."

"And it matters to me. You matter to me. Always did, always will. But it was you giving me the brush-off. Look, Elly, Southern men can be . . . a li'l bit spoiled by women. I was. From the time I was about eighteen, all these girls, and their mothers, including my own, were always trying to marry me or marry me off. I was this big catch . . . and you didn't want to catch me."

"I did want to catch you, Nick. I just didn't want to marry you."

Nick looked like an angry man trying to remember he was charming. "Right. You said you needed 'time to think.' I didn't understand what there was to think about. Love me, yes or love me, no. If it was 'yes,' and it seemed to be 'yes,' what the hell . . . what was there to think about? One entire week later you left a message on my answering machine, asking me to 'ring' you. Well, I had an attack of Guy Fever. Stomped around. Groused to my buddies and my mama. 'I've proposed marriage to this damn woman and she leaves a phone message!' *Ring* you? I wanted to ring your neck! After three days you called. Asked me to come to Southwold. I did. You said you didn't believe marriage – to anyone, ever, was right for you, that you weren't sure it was right for most people. I said you had these feelings because of your father. All his marriages, girlfriends and children. You said that wasn't true. Then, right away, you said it could be. You said that 'in any event' you hated 'the whole *marriage thing.'*

"Elly, I always went around your father. I knew he was sacred ground to you. 'I'm not him,' I said. You were it for me. I knew I'd stick if you did. You said you loved me, but that you lived and worked in Southwold. You said you also loved your job, as I loved mine, and didn't want to move to Virginia. You said you wanted us to 'just be, just love.' To me, that sounded like 'I'll see you when I see you.' We made love. It was angry, the love we made. Angry with the love pushin' through the rage and the rage pushin' back. You fell asleep. I left. I didn't call. You called once, crying into my answering machine. I didn't return the call. You didn't call again. I thought, she just wants a steady date. I want more love than she's got. I want a wife, a for- ever-mate."

He sat on the edge of the bed looking both sad and relieved. Then he took both my hands in his. "Elly, you were – the love of my life. You always will be. But the life we wanted was too different. Can you understand that?"

"Yes. I am the daughter of two such people. All the love and all the differences. Not the same differences . . . but the same love." I stood, one of my hands still in one of his. "Nick, I'm very glad you're here. There is no living person I'd rather be with. There's only one problem. I've not eaten anything all day except peanuts and choco- late-covered espresso beans. There's a place on the water, strung with multicoloured hanging lanterns. Just outside the city, on Lake Bracciano. We could have wonderful fish and pasta . . . and more wine. May we do that?"

He kissed the inside of my hand. "Yes, Ellissa Major, let's do that."

Sitting across the table from Nick, with a welcome breeze coming off the lake, I waited until the fruit and coffee to ask any further personal questions.

"When did you meet . . . Annie?"

"Ten years ago. She's a journalist. Interviewed me about the Richmond Children's Centre. You'd been out of my life a long time, but I still wasn't ready. I told her about you. She stuck by me. We were good together. Not rockets, bells and whistles like you and me. Not the crazy teasing, the laughter and the long discussions . . . and not the arguments either. I do love her. Solidly, reliably . . . and now we're bound together by our Miss Lizzy. Elly, I love Lizzy more than I thought it was possible to love anybody or anything. More than you. More than my Virginia mother and my Irish father put together. More than God on a good God day. You know about fathers and daughters – well, I'm one of those daughter-drunk fathers. For as long as she wants a daddy she's got one. And her Mamma has a husband."

You can't lose if you don't mind. And there was no point in minding a result that I'd brought into being. Or being anything other than delighted that a little girl was deeply loved. You can't be left if you never said you'd stay. Which I never had, in the way Nick wanted it said, wanted it lived. As my father said when he ended it with Helena in Ireland, "Right person, wrong rooms."

When we returned to my hotel, Nick asked if I wanted him to stay the night. I wanted this very much. What I said was, "What if . . . you're telephoned at your conference hotel? From home, I mean?"

"I'll ring the desk and ask not to be disturbed. If Annie calls, I can check my messages and call her back."

"Do this a lot, do you?"

"No. Hardly ever." There it was. The part of marriage I hated most – the pretend-fidelity. That's if you're the spouse. If you're the other one, the alternate (male or female), the subcutaneous infection is caution: being unable to be openly together any place on earth, especially in the spousal city, town or country. "Hardly ever" killed the greedy needy. "Nick – this has been – extraordinary. And I am . . . extraordinarily tired. Tomorrow is going to be a huge day for me. I think I need to sleep. Alone."

"You sure?"

No, Nick. I am not sure. I want you near me, with me, in me.

"Yes," I said.

He looked sad, recovered. "I understand. You've got a long heavy journey. All I've got is a conference. Look, could we have . . . a goodbye breakfast before you fly?"

If you come near to where there's a bed, I will . . . "Yes. I'd like that. Meet me at the Alitalia counter at nine in the morning."

"Why not here at the hotel?"

"I've documents to sort for the airport. I'd love it, though, if you'd see me off. It will make the journey easier."

"Then it's what I want. See you tomorrow. Alitalia. Nine a.m."

He kissed me. Good kiss.

The bed linens had been turned down for sleep. The room had been tidied but I could still smell Nick. I curled up inside the smell and slept. Mercifully, without dreams. I didn't want dreams. I'd had dreams all day, while fully awake. The parts of dreams that could come true for these two people at this time had done so.

Nick stood smiling in front of the Alitalia counter.

"I'll check in and show my documents and we'll breakfast, yes?"

"Yes."

We looked at each other a lot, spoke very little. At his second latte, his silence turned to safe but important career-babble.

"Hey. Did I tell you I was runnin' for guv'ner of Virginia?"

"No! Nick, that's great!"

"I've done a lot with kids and the elderly. Many Virginians asked me to run. Annie and Lizzy are good with it, so we're gonna go for it."

"I . . . wish you great good luck. *Tanti auguri*, Doctor Brown."

"I wish you the same, bright-eyed Doctor Major."

I laughed. "That's how we met. At the Pets and Therapy conference. We'd been looking at each other for two days and you walked over to me during the Animals and the Single Elderly workshop, looked at my nametag and said 'Hello, bright-eyed Doctor Major.' I said 'Hello, Doctor Brown' and you took my hand and we got the hell out of there." He reached across the black marble table, put his hand on my cheek. I kissed the inside of his palm. "And I must get the hell out of here and check on Pappino."

He sighed, stood, and produced a card. "Please, Elly, stay in touch."

We both knew I wouldn't, couldn't do that. "I'll follow the election. Good luck."

"Thanks." We hugged again. He kissed my lips lightly. "Safe journey, Elly."

"You too. Now I'd better make sure no one's stolen my father. There's a small Lucite window on top of his coffin. I look through it and say 'Yes, that's him' or 'who the hell is that?' In Italian."

"Are you serious? Why all the checking? Grave robbers?"

"Yes, actually."

"Good Lord."

"It's a wonderful world." I stood up.

"Want me to come with?"

"No. Thanks for the offer, Nick, but I should do this alone." He stood, and wrapped me up in his arms. I let my cheek rest on his neck, stealing one last moment of skin-to-skin.

This time I got to see him leave me.

A Conversation
with My Father's Face

I looked through the little plastic coffin-window. As with middle-aged women who "do their face" in bad light, Papp's makeup had settled, toned down. He looked less like the late Anna Magnani (though the lips were still too pink, and mascara on his long lashes was always going to look like drag).

The mortuary passport rested on his chest, just under the knot of a burgundy tie. It had been opened to birth-death information and a black and white photograph, taken after his embalming. The document was anchored in place by the large and rock-rigid yellow-white fingers of his well-manicured waxed hands. The photo looked like pictures of dead American cowboy bank robbers: Jesse James. Billy the Kid. Johnny Major. I remained grateful for the creepy picture and waxy cosmetics. They still helped distance me from loss – to be the strong daughter I believed Pappino would want – to protect my protector.

"Well, Pappino mio," I half-whispered, tapping lightly on the plastic window, "until I was forty, you scared away anybody who looked like he could take me from you. You did. You know you did. You wanted me to 'date' – it proved that your daughter was desirable. But you liked it that the two men I loved best were you and the son you made. Then, after the parade of suitors slowed down, you had too much red wine one night and said 'Ellissina, you should fuck more.' And I said – remember – I said 'You mean like you do?' And you said 'Well, maybe not that much,' and we both laughed. Well, I've just been fucking. And it was really and truly wonderful. You'll never guess with whom! Remember Nick Brown? The southern American. You called him 'A lightweight. All charm and no chequebook.' Well, he's running for governor of Virginia, Papp. I think he'll win – he says 'when I' about winning, not 'if I.' Like you – a 'when-guy,' not an 'if-guy.' And I've a feeling that one day he'll run for bloody president of the United bloody States! And I've just been fucking him! And it was . . ."

There was throat-clearing behind me. I turned, and saw two ground-crew men in bright yellow jumpsuits. "*Scusi, signora,*" one said, looking down at his feet. The other explained that they had to take the body to the plane. I apologised for having taken so long, but that I had wanted to talk to my father. This made the shorter man laugh. His mate slapped him on the upper arm, hissing "Ssh, '*dzito!*" They closed the coffin and carried the coffin from yet another cold room, twitchy lips still suppressing laughter.

Were they laughing at the idiot-woman nattering at a dead man's face inside a sealed coffin, or was 'fuck' one of those English words known all over the world, even to the most unilingual? Realising that I would not have an answer to this profound question any time soon, I headed to gate 22 and flight 334.

PAPPINO, LIDDRU AND
A BAG OF RICE BALLS

We landed bumpily on the Palermo airstrip. The Sicilian passengers applauded. This made me smile and I applauded with them.

To my jet-lagged eyes, the luggage carousel was a buzzing, flapping nest of flies and bats – black-clad wives and grandmothers, their bags and boxes tied round with heavy rope. These containers were chirped at, pointed to and grabbed as they revolved, to be hauled up and away by dutiful husbands and sons. Huge-eyed kids were running everywhere, laughing, screaming and playing finger-as-gun games. It was a relief to have only a carry-on bag. I reclaimed my potentially lethal Swiss Army Knife, untaped this time, due to the apparent fearlessness of the Italian authorities, and was told where to collect Pappino's coffin. In the passenger hall, I scanned the gauntlet of cardboard cards for my name. There it was, in large handmade black lettering: *Signora Maggiore*.

Above the sign was the smiling, sparsely toothed, largely nosed little face of a man who appeared to be about a hundred and four years old. A grey coat hung from his sloping shoulders, almost to the ground. A battered hat, of darker grey, sat atop his head. I waved to him, mouthing the word "Liddru?"

"*Si, si, si,*" he mouthed back, raising his hat twice before moving slowly towards me, smiling, chopping his hand up and down in welcome, rather as the Pope did on telly. His voice was brittle and nasal: "Ellissa? *Dottore* Ellissa Maggiore?"

"*Si.*"

He reached up, cupping my face in small dry hands. *"Brava. Benvenuta. Benvenuta é condolianze per il papá tuo!"*

I thanked him for his welcome, and for his sympathy.

Apart from my father, I'd never been in a car driven by someone over eighty. In his last years, a few dings and fender-benders had called Papp's driving into question, but so strong and focused was the force of his personality that he always (if not always wisely) prevailed in court, and drove until shortly before his final hospitalisation.

Two airport workers placed the coffin in the back of Liddru's large black station wagon. I'd expected a hearse. In a station wagon, the coffin was sort of "free standing," so I asked to sit in back with it, in case we hit a bump in the road. Liddru nodded, handing me a somewhat oily brown bag. *"Arangini,"* he said. Rice balls. There were, he proudly informed me in dialect, rice balls, spiced olives and biscotti. All made by Rosalba, his youngest daughter. Also a jar of homemade wine from his grapes, Agrigento grapes.

"You like rice balls?"

I told him I loved rice balls (which I did). He said that my father had also loved rice balls (which I knew).

Exhausted by the unusually eventful Roman leg of my journey, I felt it might be best, if possible, to sleep through Liddru's driving. Climbing into the back of the wagon, I curled up with my legs over Papp's coffin, cradling my bag of rice balls until we reached Agrigento, where I was awakened by the bleating of the goats.

LA SICILIA E LA FAMIGLIA

We were in the middle of the town-square, alongside a cherub-encrusted fountain, our car surrounded by fifteen or twenty flop-eared goats. Shaking myself awake, I grinned and giggled. *"Capre!"* I cried. Since childhood, I had loved Italian goats.

"Si, si, capre. Goat! You like goat?"

"Si. I love goat!"

"Your mother is also here," said my mother the bollard, opening the back of the station wagon, "but if you want to first greet the goats . . ."

"Ciao, Mammina," I replied, climbing out and hugging my mother, who, as always, went rigid inside my embrace.

Auntie Nan, with whom I'd always associated colourful clothes, lipstick and cigarettes, looked old and pale in a shapeless black dress and absence of make-up. Her white hair, usually set in a style reminiscent of Queen Elizabeth, had been combed straight back and into a bun at the nape of her neck. The severe hairdo was partially covered by a black lace headscarf. She hugged me, saying *"Benvenuto,* Ellissina" in a teary broken rasp. I could feel the shakiness in her frail body and hugged her in return, saying, in Sicilian, "I love you, *Zia* Antoinetta. I am here for you."

Liddru stood at my side, grinning, nodding and softly making those southern Italian sounds that are not quite words – mmo, boh, beh, ngah. He was a super driver, I thought, whatever his age, as I had slept soundly throughout our entire two-hour journey from Palermo.

"Bravo, *Signor* Liddru!" I said, going on to praise his driving, and being rewarded by a pinch on both cheeks and a huge gummy grin.

No bollard he, I thought, taking his right hand in both of mine. "You are a very fine man, and I thank you for what you have done today for me, and for my father," I said, feeling the Sloppy Woppy that was my birthright begin to displace English imprinting.

Liddru, having no imprint but Agrigento, responded in kind: "Thank you, *Dottore* Ellissina, for the words you say to me today. Your father, Don Giovanni Paolo Maggiore, was a great man, a man who carried the name of Agrigento into the world. A respected man, a man of honour, a man who . . ."

"*Basta*, Liddru!" said Mammina. "There will be time for speeches. Now, we must take Vanni up to the house. Also, my little girl has travelled very far, and must change her clothes and wash herself."

Liddru agreed that my mother's fifty-year-old little girl should do all that had been proposed. Men, who'd been standing amongst the goats, came forward and lifted the coffin out of the car. It was a grey windy day. Light drizzle had begun to fall. Four men bore the coffin through narrow streets (watched by Agrigentian eyes peeping through time-beiged gauzy curtains), past the stone church, which looked as I remembered it – the creamy pink-white colour of a bleached conch shell. Some, including my mother and aunt, crossed themselves, and then we headed up a rocky hillside to my father's childhood home, now home to Cousin Giuseppino, a widower whose wife Anna, whom I'd never met, had died a few years earlier of throat cancer.

The house, near the top of the hill, overlooking the Mediterranean, had only three rooms, a large one downstairs and two upstairs. They were many-purposed, these ochre-yellow-walled rooms – but only three.

Pappino had first brought me to this house when I was nine, wanting me to "see what you come from, see the house, smell the smells, breathe the air of Agrigento."

"It's so small,"I had said, with the tact and grace of a snobbish urban English nine-year-old. "Not for Agrigento," Pappino replied. "In

Agrigento, in most Sicilian towns, a small house is one room, plus a shed or a barn, and a *bacowz* – an outhouse. This house is *una mezzacasa*, a medium-sized house. One is privileged to have a *mezzacasa*. My father earned the price of a *mezzacasa* because he ran the pharmacy . . ."

"The same as he did in Montréal."

"Exactly. He had to take all new Canadian classes and tests so he could be a Canadian pharmacist. He was very determined, your *Nonnu*. He always did what he had to do."

Nine-year-old me took in the big downstairs room cluttered with an accretion of pictures and objects on the wall, furniture, rugs scattered on the wooden floor. The room comprised a kitchen, a bathtub and a parlour. There were two old wooden-framed fabric screens – one to separate the kitchen from the parlour, the other to modestly block the bathtub. The one for the kitchen/parlour division depicted three round-faced large-eyed, pink-cheeked 19th-century girls in off-white confirmation dresses with pink or pale blue cummerbunds, white stockings and pink shoes. They smiled shyly with pale tinted raspberry lips, their blonde or brunette hair falling in cylindrical ringlets to just above their well-covered full breasts. The screen shielding the claw-foot bathtub was a heavier, nubbier fabric in floral design – red and yellow roses and green leaves, against a cream background.

"Are there no houses in Agrigento any bigger than three rooms?"

"Yes, Ellissina, there are some villas. They belong to people whose ancestors inherited them from conquerors, or in civil wars. Others made money in America or elsewhere in Italy or the world, then came back and bought villas to die in, or leave to their children. One villa is always given by the government to the prefect for the area. Another, the biggest one in town, belongs to an old friend of mine. He is like an un-elected official. He takes care of . . . the daily problems of the people who live here. We will dine with him this evening, in his very grand Sicilian villa."

Standing there weary and wet, so many years later, I could see and hear my younger father as if he had been had been filmed and recorded with perfect clarity. While I was doing all this other-time seeing and hearing, my mother's little girl had been saying *"piaceri, molto piaceri"* to various "uzza," "ino," "ina," and "iddu" people, all of whom were being presented to *Dottore* Ellissa Maggiore, the daughter of Don Giovanni Paolo.

At the end of the queue was Cousin Giuseppino, son to one of the two brothers of Nannu Dominicu who had died in the Second World War. We'd met before, in Agrigento when we were children. As an adult, about five years older than I, he had the family hair and face, a thinner version of my father's face. My eyes filled. *"Gugino* Giuseppe," I said softly, throwing my arms around him. He returned the hug. People applauded and laughed.

"Iddra gonuushe!" Liddru cried. "She knows him! She does not see him for many years, but she knows him without hearing his name!"

Though I was fully attired in the mourning colour, Mammina said I should go upstairs to "the little bedroom" and change to black clothes that were fresh and dry.

I recognised the little bedroom; years earlier it had been a large walk-in clothes cupboard. It contained a narrow bed, bedside table and table lamp, two-drawer wooden dresser with oval mirror attached and a wooden chair.

I peeled off damp clothes, opened my wheely-bag and pulled out a stretchy black wool sheath dress. My tights should have been black as well, but, hurriedly, I'd packed a colour called "Suntan." Suntan would have to do. My running shoes, good for climbing the rocky hills of Agrigento, were black. They were also running shoes. I hoped no one would be offended. My hair was still damp. I'd brought a dryer and an adapter for the change of current, but felt the whirring noise would be inappropriate. Sitting on the floor towelling my hair with the bottom of the white chenille bedspread wasn't wildly appropriate either, but seemed the best option. The funereal makeover was completed by red lipstick – first put on and then wiped off, for a touch of colour. I blended a bit of this lipstick into my cheeks and regarded myself in the mirror:

"Oh, Pappino mio, I've never done this before. Be with me. Don't let me disgrace you."

A carved wooden Jesus, the size of my shoe, was crucified on the wall, above the tiny bed. For the first time since childhood, I crossed myself, took a deep breath, exhaled and headed down the varnished wooden steps, holding firmly to the railing.

SOME SPEAK, SOME SCREAM

My father's coffin occupied the centre of the parlour floor, on a wooden table atop a Turkish-style mostly red rug. The lid lay alongside the coffin. Reflexively, I looked away. I'd loved my father's face all my life, and did not want it superceded in memory by this embalmed head with its rouge and mascara, surgical scars glowing white behind the ears and around the eyes. The others, seeing post-mortem Pappino for the first time, crowded around, chattering in dialect, voicing their traditional disapproval of embalming. Mammina said it was Canadian law for travelling corpses. Carlino Giambraccini, the local tailor, said embalming was not Sicilian, and that it was *"carcinogenico."*

"Carcinogenico? What the hell is that?"

"Cancer. Embalming fluid causes cancer."

"Cancer? The man is dead, Lino. Cancer won't bother him."

"What about us? The fluid could give us cancer."

"Don't kiss him. You'll be fine if you don't kiss him."

At one point, annoyed by yet another particularly insistent complainer, she snapped "Listen, *testa di googootz*, if they hadn't done him up this way, he'd stink like hell by now!"

Outside the window, it was dark, with a big moon and low-hanging stars. I moved to go outside for a bit of air. Mammina rushed to my side, whispering, "No, Ellissina, you can't leave."

"Why not? I'm not going away, I just . . ."

"No, you have to stay in the house until Vanni's soul flies up to heaven."

"Oh. How long . . . does that usually take?"

"Two days. Forty-eight hours. No eating, no sleeping. Just here, on the chairs, with the speeches and the screaming. It is the tradition."

"What if I have to go . . . ?"

"The outhouse. If you absolutely have to. Put this in your purse." She pressed a wad of paper into my hand. Having left my handbag upstairs, I crammed it into my running shoe, as quickly and subtly as one can shove a clump of toilet paper into a shoe.

It had stopped drizzling, which was good, since all the windows were open so Pappino could fly to heaven (a large woman whispered something about the relationship between heaven and my father's divorces, and the man beside her, also large, told her to shut up). Wooden chairs with woven rush-matting seats had been placed around the coffin. The immediate family, including Cousin Giuseppino, his sister Carmelina, Auntie Nan, Mammina and me were brought to sit in these chairs. Mammina's familial immediacy could have been considered a bit dodgy due to her divorce and remarriage, but this appeared to have been resolved amongst the Maggiore relatives. Probably because, of all Pappino's wives, she was the first, and more importantly, the only *Siciliana*. Two somewhat wild-eyed and softly moaning old women had also been seated.

Mammina, next to me, whispered that "we have to make speeches about Vanni now. In Sicilian. You can do this, yes?"

"Yes."

"*Bene*. You will be the last from the sitting people. Then others from the town will speak. The women will scream between the speeches . . ."

"They will scream?"

"*Si*. They are *giangiulini* – traditional screamers. Every town in Sicily has them. They are paid to scream."

"Paid to scream?"

"I'll explain later. Try not to jump when they scream. It can be very loud. I have less to say, so I will make the first speech."

She walked to the coffin, looked inside, murmured something, and then turned to face us. Her eyes, for one of the few times ever in my memory, filled with tears. She quickly wiped them away and spoke. Her voice was strong and clear. Both hands rested on her chest above her breasts – right hand over left, fingers, perhaps unconsciously, covering the wedding band of her marriage to Doug:

"I loved this man always. I love him now. We could not live together. We were too much the same. A room with Giovanni Paolo Maggiore in it, when he was alive, had room for only one such person. He built his own success, started from almost nothing. No money, no connections – only his dreams and the dreams of his father, Don Dominicu Maggiore. Giovanni Paolo Maggiore was somebody in this world. He did things, he made things. Nothing, no man or woman on earth, no thieves, no liars, could stop him. Not then, while he lived, and not now. People honoured him. We honour him now. He was a wonderful father to our daughter, Ellissa Giovanna, who is with us today, who also honours him here. Be with God now, Vanni."

As Mammina had warned, when she stopped speaking the two women started beating their breasts and screaming; piercing, brain-lancing wails unlike any I'd ever heard. If there were devils, demons or Dutch people planning to fuck with my father's final glide path, they were being mightily warned against it. Listening to the howls of the two hired mourners, I, who wanted nothing but joy and glory for my father, forever and ever, world without end, was terrified by the sound. Without Mammina having alerted me, I think my own heart might've stopped.

Liddru spoke next. He declared that it was a privilege and honour to have been a friend of Giovanni Paolo Maggiore since they were Agrigentese children and how Don Giovanni sent money to him for years to care for Ntoniu, Liddru's badly crippled son, who still could not walk but was a smart boy who loved to read and went to university in Palermo, thanks to Don Giovanni Paolo, and now taught music and Italian history in the Agrigento High School.

Perhaps because Liddru had an older and quieter voice than my mother, the wailing women screamed at intervals during his speech as well as afterwards. Liddru, used to Sicilian rituals, spoke without flinching without pause and without punctuation, until he had said all he wished to say. He would speak again in Pappino's ascension process. Over the next two foodless drinkless days, my mother and I would be the only mourners to speak only once.

After Liddru, Cousin Giuseppino spoke. I learned that my father had supported him until he became the town's best carpenter, making the chairs on which we were seated. Thanks to my father, he and his two sons, Giovannino and Corrado, had become skilled and valued enough to have made, for twenty-five years, most of the wooden tables and chairs in Agrigento. Giovannino and Corrado, who looked like their father, and therefore like mine, made little head-bows when their names were mentioned, and the two old women screamed for a bit. We'd only been at this ritual for about two hours. Forty-six to go. I looked at my mother.

"Learn to sleep with your eyes open," she whispered in English.

"Through the screaming?"

"Yes."

Night changed to day and then to night again. The people – friends, relatives, ancient schoolmates – most of them unknown to me, spoke of my father's good deeds. If they were to be believed, and there was no reason they should not be, Pappino had, over the years, supported half the town.

I went twice to the outhouse. Having had no food or drink, these trips were only for needed air and a break from speeches and screaming. Returning from my second excursion, I was informed that, after Carmelina and Stellario, it would be my turn to speak.

Cousin Carmelina thanked my father for her eyeglasses, and for those of her two daughters, who, sadly, had inherited her bad eyes.

Stellario, who'd returned to Agrigento two days earlier, in order to honour my father, was pit boss in the casino of the London Cognoscenti. He thanked "my employer and my great friend" for "my fantastic job," and for introducing him to his beautiful, blonde English wife, Emma, whom he'd met when she was working at the club as a singer and blackjack dealer. He also thanked him for his three children, Stella, Samantha and Nigel. I was not sure what part Pappino had played in the birth of Stellario's children but knew better than to ask.

When Stellario finished his eulogy and the women had screamed (by this time, a bit hoarsely), he gestured towards me, and said, in dialect, "I present now *Dottore* Ellissa Giovanna Maggiore, first-born child of Don Giovanni, whom I have known since she was a small girl in London. *Ragazzina!*"

I walked to the coffin. Bending my face into it, I kissed my father lightly. He smelled of talcum powder and, I thought, sawdust. I then stood alongside, rather than in front of the coffin, holding onto its brass handle. Feeling shaky, I did this for balance – but also in hope that Pappino's perfect Sicilian would flow from the top of his head through the coffin into my hand and up my arm, until it reached my brain, and, from there, would come out of my mouth. I had a moment of panic. Looked at Mammina, who smiled and nodded. I spoke:

"Love. Everyone everywhere uses this word. They use it for parents, for children, for husbands, wives, relatives and friends. They use it for strangers. They use it when they win prizes, when they buy something, when they sell something, when they want something, when they get something they want. They say the word 'love' when babies are born. And they say it when people die. I love you, Pappino. I always did. More accurately, I never did not. Never. Not for one moment. Even if I was mad at you, or disagreed with something you said or did, I also loved you. No matter who else or what else I loved, loving *you* was always at the core of my heart. Always. And I knew, from the moment I knew things, that you loved me. How could I not know? I lived inside that love, as if it were my invisible house. The house that was your love protected me, no matter where I was, no matter what I was doing. And I always knew how to reach you, knew I could come to you, could ask you to come to me. I did not ask you to come to me very often – I can only remember two times. What was important, what made my invisible house so warm, so safe, was that I knew I could ask. And that you would come.

"Dear family and friends, I do have an actual house. It is a fine house, a *mezzacasa*, in a part of England called Suffolk. Across the road from that house, where my father would visit me many times, I have my work. I am what, in English, is called 'a small-animal veterinarian' – dogs, cats, birds, rabbits. Mostly dogs and cats. I believe I chose this work because of my father. You all know him – even though he always said that no one really knew him – that no one could really know anybody. You all remember how often he spoke of being cunning and wise and watchful with people – being what he called *furba*.

"There were very few people my father trusted. Always, he told me 'you can like people, you can even love them, but do not trust them.' He said, 'people do not always intend to betray other people – they, we, simply cannot help it. We are humans, and humans are still savages. So you also, Ellissina,' he said, 'you may betray somebody. Me also' he said, 'I have betrayed people. Not many. But I know I have done it. The betrayal demon comes, and you obey this demon. It happens, because it is in the blood of all humans for it to happen. So you must be *furba* – cunning, watchful – with everyone – even friends and family.'

"I cannot be as *furba* as my father. Few people can. Instead, I chose to work with domesticated animals. Because, when you know them, unless something has driven them crazy-mad, they can be trusted.

"My brother Davy – Giovanni Davide Maggiore – is one of the people my father trusted. He is a wonderful brother and was a wonderful son. When Pappino was sick in Montréal, in his last days, Davy came from England to be at his bedside. Davy would be with us now, but he is an actor, a fine actor – in London. And making a beautiful film. A film for little children. His producers have a contract with him and said he could not leave. He will come to Agrigento as soon as he is free to travel, and he will go to our father's grave to pay his respect. To honour our father. He will do this with love.

"I cannot imagine my life without the house that was my father. But I will have to learn. We will all have to learn. We must now build our own invisible houses, knowing that he will visit us there. Whenever he wants to. And I hope, oh God, I hope, whenever we want and need him to. *Benedetto, Pappino mio. Io te amo, ora e sempre!*"

When I finished speaking, there was more screaming, now from five or six women. And then some of those who were standing behind our ring of chairs came forward. They each praised my father; some briefly, others at length. The speaking and screaming continued into the following morning, when, from outside the house, there came the loud music of a brass band. Everyone stood, and Cousin Giuseppino went to the door. Standing there were about twenty teenagers, all playing musical instruments, conducted by a small man seated in a wheelchair.

Liddru's son, Ntoniu.

PROCESSIONE

Two men closed Pappino's coffin, and, joined by two others, carried it out of the house. The screaming women were now waving their arms above their heads, wailing as if they were being stabbed. Mammina, seeing me momentarily frozen by the increased intensity and volume, grabbed and squeezed my hand, leading me outside.

The young musicians, winter sun glinting off their instruments, had that large-eyed combination of gravity and yearning openness one frequently sees in Greco-Italian Sicilian children. For me, at that moment, in that place, they were pacifying faces; faces filled with hope born of not yet knowing much of the world. I hope you keep your hope, *picciliddi*, I thought, flooding with affection for them – flooding with love.That love and my mother's hand in mine extinguished my fear as we took our places behind the coffin.

Someone shouted N'*dindiimu! Processione!* and we wove down the hill and through the narrow streets to the church. The music – exultant, majestic and sombre – accompanied our journey. Its melody, played in the staccato favoured by school-aged musicians, made me think of a fireworks display, exploding in colours, seen from the top of a hill, the bass drum like a fist beating repeatedly from inside a huge heart: Bam! Bam! Bam! Bam! La, Loolie La, Loolie La, Looloodie La, Looloodie La! Bam! Bam! Bam! Bam!

People came out of their houses and joined our throng, some of them screaming. At one point I realised that I too had started to scream, tears rolling down my face as I held tightly to Mammina's hand. Our procession stopped, one or two rows at a time, in front of the church. There were two rounded belfries at the top of the church, seemingly made of stone openwork lace and pinky-white cement cake icing. Each belfry housed a large bell. Both bells were ringing. I stopped screaming, looking through a teary blur at the church door, then up to the bells and sky.

Oh my, I thought, oh my, Ellissa Giovanna Maggiore. You thought you knew The Full Sloppy Woppy! You knew *nenti*! This is The Full Sloppy Woppy! This is a Sloppy Woppy as big as the world – bigger even than Giovanni Paolo Maggiore, who, until this moment, was the biggest thing you knew!

My legs were wobbly but we were so tightly packed as we headed up the church steps that I had nowhere to fall and no way of falling unless I fainted. There was so much oxygen in the cool air, so much energy pulsing through the millipede we had become that I knew I was not going to faint.

BASTINA IN AGRIGENTO

The inside of the old stone church smelled of incense, candle-wax, oiled wood and mildew dampness. Mammina and I were seated in the first row of wooden pews. My father's coffin, still closed, was placed on a raised altar behind the priest, who was in white and gold. He had a strong big face and lion-mane silver hair. I wondered if he were a Maggiore.

I could hear him speak, hear the sounds, interlaced with women screaming from various parts of the church, but my brain had emptied. I had become what my parents called *testa di Djadrool* – a pumpkinhead. A hollowed-out gourd. Ellissa the Gourd sat calmly, hands folded in lap. A good little girl. A *ragazzina perfetta*. I understood not a word, except the name Giovanni Paolo Maggiore and isolated words of affirmation or identification – *benedetto, bravo, fratello, famiglia.*

It wasn't the dialect. At that point, I would not have understood any language except for random words. When a familiar word would come, I felt warmed by it, but did not try to hold it. Pumpkinhead sat next to her mother, smiling slightly. As I had since childhood, I could feel Bastina coming. Coming as she always did when it all overloaded, coming to keep me from breaking into a thousand bits of broken coloured glass. Bastina, my secret self, named by my father and known only to that father and this daughter.

The words of the priest, the murmurs of the townspeople, the paid screamers – all sounded very far away. Bastina entered my body. I smiled. My name is Bastina, I thought. I am called Bastina because. Sometimes. I must. Just. Stop.

Sermon concluded, the coffin was lifted again. The cemetery, I thought. We are going to the cemetery. No. Bastina does not want to do that now. Bastina wants to do that tomorrow. Alone. Bastina will faint now.

And I did. Not a fake faint, a true one. My mother, who, better than most, understands acts of pure will, would tell me later that she'd said "Take her to Giuseppino's house and put her in the bed in the little bedroom." She asked one of the women to undress me and put me in warm clothes, covering me with two blankets. She told them to put a pitcher of water and a glass on the chair next to the bed. She said I would be fine, that everything had just been *un po di troppo*, a bit too much.

A large man who smelled of cigarettes carried me back to Cousin Giuseppino's. He had my limp arms gathered in, my head resting against his scratchy vest. Half-awake by then, I opened my eyes for a moment. Blue-grey sky and candyfloss clouds. Our path was bumpy but I did not believe the man would stumble or that I would be dropped. I closed my eyes again, pleased to be carried – a coffinless imitation of my father.

A VISITOR FROM THE SKY

Ragdoll Ragazzina, I let the women undress me and tuck me into the narrow bed, murmuring an occasional *grazie, grazie tante per tutto*, to let them know I was not delirious.

In the middle of the night, I was awakened by Pappino. He wore a long white caftan-like garment, was barefoot and flew just above the house, calling my name, "Ellissina, Ellissina!"

I tiptoed out of bed and went to the open window. I was wearing an unfamiliar white flannel nightdress. The air was cold, damp. Sea air. Pappino hovered like an enormous hummingbird, just above the open window and just out of reach. I waved, grinning. "Ciao, Pappino mio! Oh my, look at you! Aren't you cold?"

"No. Cold doesn't exist once you die."

"Oh? Did you see that film, *Truly, Madly, Deeply?* The English film by an Anglo-Italian. Minghella. In the film, dead people wear coats and scarves and things all the time because they're always cold."

"That's a film. This is death. And not being cold is one of the good parts. You also get to keep . . . your erection."

I couldn't help it. I laughed. "Your erection? All the time?"

"No, just so much that you know you get to keep it."

"I've never had an erection to keep, Papp. Will I get one when I die?"

It was his turn to laugh. "Probably not. I don't know . . . how any of that works here yet. And, erection or no, I'm not sure I want to know. It's like not being cold – things may be easier without erections. I'm not sure I want to fly around with half a hard-on until the end of time. Maybe, though, not doing sex in the way we do when we're alive will be more . . . peaceful, will be one of the good parts."

"Do you know yet what the bad parts are?"

"No. I don't know much, Ellissina. Haven't even been able to find out who's in charge."

"In charge? God, no? Lord Jesus? Some of his people?"

"Yeah, all that, at least in the Christian Sector . . . but I haven't got it sorted out yet. I only know that there are a large number of different gods and goddesses here. That part, I think, is like on earth. And the top people have others who work for them. Also like on earth. Nobody has told me where to report. The two guys who welcomed me said somebody is going to tell me, but it hasn't happened yet."

"Two guys? Angels?"

"Dunno. Don't think so. No wings. But they were flying around, like I am now. I think everyone here flies."

"I hope nobody's going to try giving you orders."

He laughed. "Yeah, me too. I hope orders are like cold weather. It stops when you die, and you just work it out or walk away. They have given me this list of things I can do. It's like Open University classes in England. Here, wherever 'here' is, you're supposed to choose things you've never done before. I may take up art. Sculpture."

"Really? You? I didn't know you were interested in . . . that sort of thing."

"Yeah, always wanted to try sculpting. Never had time before. Now, if I've got this new thing figured out correctly, I'm gonna have nothing but time. And I do like the flying. The flying is great!"

"I've always wanted to fly. Not in a plane – to fly the way birds do."

"Everyone wants that, I think, to fly like a bird. That reminds me, be careful with the Dutch bird."

"Dutch bird? You mean Petra?"

"Yes. *Adasciu, adasciu,* Ellissina. *Furba.*"

There, above the window, both his image and his voice were becoming faint.

"You're fading, Pappino. I'm losing you."

"Yeah. They told me about the fading business. But you'll never lose me, Ellissina mia. Like what you asked for beside my coffin, I will try always to show up for you. If I don't, it will mean there's some sort of red tape holding me up, but I'll get to you as soon as I can. And tell your mother I heard what she said. About loving me always. Tell her . . . tell her I never stopped loving her. And never will. And your brother, tell your brother, you know . . ."

"Davy."

"Yes, John David. Tell him I'll see him when he comes to the cemetery. Tell him I will be able to see him whether he can see me or not. And that I love him. And that I'm sorry I used that word when he was a kid. Tell him the Agrigentese are . . ."

And he was gone; at least gone from where I could see and hear him. I went back to bed. Shivering a bit, I pulled the two blankets over me, up to just below my closing eyes. Oh, Sicily, I thought. You are a tiny planet between this world and some other one. I slept again.

Just before dawn, in the grey-light, I awoke in the narrow bed. My mother sat on the floor in a nest of sheets and blankets, looking up at me.

"Mammina, what are you doing on the floor?"

"You fainted at the church. I thought you'd better have the bed."

"No, the bed should be for you . . ."

"I'm fine here, Ellissina. My bed at home is very hard. I like it that way. Doug always says our bed is like sleeping on the floor."

I turned on the bed-lamp. "We could both sleep in the bed."

"No. It's too small. I toss a lot in my sleep. I didn't want to swing my arm out and hurt you. One night, in Victoria, I swung my arm out in my sleep and gave Doug a bloody nose. So we got a bigger bed. King-size. And Doug sleeps facing away from me, so that the worst I can do is punch him in the back."

I laughed. "Yeh, I toss and swing out too."

"You also talk in your sleep. I don't do that. It's why I woke up. I heard you."

I poured some water from the pitcher by the bed. "What was I saying?"

"I couldn't make it out. I think you were talking to your father. Were you dreaming of him?"

"Yes."

"I thought so. Can you remember it?"

"Not exactly. He seemed all right, though. He looked good. He could fly. Like birds fly."

Mammina smiled. "I bet he liked that, being able to fly."

"Yeh. He said he did. I remember that. The rest is sort of blurry. Maybe it'll come back."

"I hope so. If the dream come back, will you tell me?"

"Of course."

I looked down at my nightdress. White flannel, long. I had never seen it before. Except in my dream. I remembered every millimoment of that dream. I just wasn't ready to talk about it, wasn't ready for my mother's questions, for her wondering, as I did, whether I'd had a dream or some sort of visit.

THE BAD TOWN

Daylight came. Mammina, carrying a pitcher and bowl, and wearing a dark blue woollen robe, headed downstairs for hot water. I stared out the recently father-filled window, thinking again about my childhood visit to Agrigento. And about the bad town.

Pappino had said we'd spend the day driving around Sicily. One of the 'Freedom and Choices' trips we both loved. "Super!" I shouted.

Mariuzza, the neighbour who cooked for us, had fixed a basket of food, including about eight rice balls, broccoli rapini, spiced olives and hard little s-shaped biscotti – plus wine for Pappino, orange fizzy-water for me, and mineral water for us both.

It was a wonderful day. Pappino told stories of things that happened to him as an Agrigentese boy. We wandered through ancient Greek temples, visited Muslim and Viking sites, played in the sea, ate rice balls and sang in the car. Pappino had a good voice for Southern Italian songs – "Cuor' 'Ngrato," "Diciticello Vuoia," "Mamma" – the Sloppy Woppy Greatest Hits rolled out of the open car windows and into the land of our ancestors. By late afternoon, we were in the foothills of a mountain village. Papp began driving up the narrow rocky road to the town. As soon as we entered the piazza, I started pleading with him to turn round, to go back, to leave the town.

"Please, Pappino! I don't want to stay here! I'm afraid!"

He looked at me gravely. "Afraid? What are you afraid of Ellissina?"

"I don't know. I'm just afraid. This is . . . a bad place."

He held my face in his hands, his eyes were darkest brown and very bright. "Good, Ellissina. *Brava*. This is a bad place. We go."

He turned the car around and we left the town, which was slowly being enveloped in heavy glossy darkness. Later, I would describe this shiny murk as "sticky."

I didn't want to talk for awhile, so I pretended to sleep. Pappino knew I was pretending, and said, in dialect, that everything would be all right. That he would not let anything bad happen to me. That he would never let anything bad happen to me.

When we were back in Agrigento, safe in the house, he told me about the dark mountain town – that there had been gang wars there, between two families, for many years. Many people were murdered. People were still murdered there, because of continuing blood feuds.

"That town, Ellissina, is like the *Coliseo* in Rome. That Coliseum is full of little wild cats waiting for the lions to come back, and there is too much blood under the ground."

"Why did you take me there, to a bad town?"

He smiled, rubbing his index finger against my cheek. "I wanted to see if you'd recognise a bad town. It's important for you to recognise such things, for you to leave such places. Or, if you must stay, to know what sort of place you are in, to get out as fast as possible – to keep your back to the wall and watch the door."

To this day, I never sit anywhere with my back to the door, unless I think a person with me can watch that door. A person like my father or my mother. Not Davy. Davy would have no idea what to watch for. He isn't Sicilian enough. When we're out somewhere, I cover Davy. I don't discuss it; I just do it.

TEARS, LAUGHTER
AND CELESTIAL RED TAPE

Given my absence, by fainting on the previous day, I knew it was time, for my solitary trip to Pappino's grave.

A photo of Pappino, in an onyx and gilt oval frame, protected by Plexiglas, was embedded in his gravestone, just above his name, his birth-date in Agrigento, Sicilia and death-date in Montréale, Canada. It was the same twenty-year-old photo that had accompanied his Montréal obituaries. A theatrical photographer friend of Mareike's had taken it. "They light you from below, these show-business photographers," he said at the time. "Takes every line and bag out of your face." Lineless and bagless, the sixty-nine-year-old Johnny Major looked at me from the eighty-nine-year-old Giovanni Paolo Maggiore's gravestone.

The cemetery was a dry lopsided place, on a rocky lumpy hillside. There were many flowers. The real ones, yellow, red or white, were scattered atop freshly settling earth. The plastic ones, bright and shiny, with hard little petals of fuschia-pink, red or turquoise and equally hard leaves of dark green, sprouted from cups, bottles and jars. Pappino's white gravestone sat between the pale mottled grey ones of his father, Dominicu Angelo Maggiore, and his mother Cecilia Giambalvo Maggiore. I knew *Nonna* Maggiore only from stories told by my father and Auntie Nan. I knew her as perfect in every way, made so by the non-contradiction death provides. I touched both gravestones, offering a granddaughter's greeting, before speaking to the larger alabaster stone standing between them.

"Pappino? Are you here now? Apart from the body in the coffin?" Sounds of wind, of rustling leaves in trees. Far below, the sound of the sea and seabirds.

"Were you here last night? Flying? Was that a dream? Are you having . . . red tape now?" I laughed. "Red tape" had always been one of Papp's expressions. Could death be actually followed by red tape? Shouldn't red tape be like cold weather, non-existent for the dead? Or are there so many Dead that the red tape is even worse? I had thought, the previous evening, to tell him about the missing will, but knew that he would be angry. He had said that death evaporated anger, but, happy to see him, in a dream or otherwise, I was unwilling to spoil the moment with "business."

Davy, who had lost many friends to AIDS, once said that "the ones who really care don't cry right away. We keep it together. We do what has to be done. We don't embarrass ourselves. We don't embarrass the dead. But then, when the witnesses are gone, usually suddenly, usually when looking at the moon, we go. We howl, we wail."

There was no moon at Pappino's gravesite. Only blue sky, floating clouds and, way below, the sea and sand. Alone, with no obligation to present myself as Strong Daughter of Strong Father, I howled with weeping.

RIDING A BLIND DOG HOME

Howled out and hollow, I walked slowly back to Giuseppino's. I needed to leave Sicily, to get back to our damn scavenger hunt, but had no idea when the rules of tradition would permit this. An hour later, the answer came from Stellario, my father's London casino manager.

The assembled family and friends were as I had left them – eating, drinking, sharing stories. Stellario was telling about a famous Hollywood star who had not paid his casino debts. My father arranged to have Stellario visit the actor on the set of a big expensive film. There, in front of a full cast and crew – about three hundred people – Stellario said, "loud, but with dignity, Good afternoon Ladies and Gentlemen. I apologise for interrupting your work. I am here in behalf of Mister Johnny Major, owner of London's Cognoscenti Club and Casino, with which many of you are familiar. Your great star, Mister Kevin Day, a man Mister Major much admires as a great artist, has a long-standing unpaid bill at the casino. Cognoscenti is in the middle of some very costly renovations, renovations being made for the pleasure of Mister Day and our many other fine guests. Therefore, with the kind co-operation of Mister Arthur Globerman, the producer of this film, I have been permitted to interrupt your work so that I can collect a cheque from Mister Day for two hundred thousand, five hundred and fifty-two dollars, U.S. – the sum that is owed. This is an exact sum, with no interest charged, as a courtesy to Mister Day, who is one of Mister Major's favourite actors. Mister Major deeply regrets any embarrassment my visit may cause Mister Day, whom he truly admires, but our three prior written requests have gone unanswered.

"Well, Kevin Day, who was wearing a toga and sandals at the time, comes to the centre of the room and, in this big fancy voice like a priest, he says, 'Oh, my good man. Has that not been attended to? I've recently changed personal assistants and Ricky' – or Dicky, something *icky*, his new boy – 'must have missed it, or it got lost in the post. Please, if you will accompany me to my dressing room, I shall write you a cheque, in the full amount.' Then the crowd parted and we went to Day's dressing room and I got Johnny Major's money!" There was applause for Stellario's story, plus cries of "Bravo, Giovanni Paolo, bravo, Stellario."

. Stellario then went on: "Ladies and Gentleman, as you know, Johnny Major, Giovanni Paolo Maggiore, was a tough man about money and waste. Well, it is in my contract with Cognoscenti Casino that I can take time off for 'a death in the family' for three days maximum. Even though the passing is now that of my beloved boss himself, Cognoscenti expects me back tomorrow. So, I must leave today for Palermo, and fly tonight from Rome to London."

Everyone said they understood. In the family tradition, I decided to Take a Shot.

"Excuse me, please, everyone, but I too have . . . a problem. Of course, as my father's daughter, I will do what you believe he would wish . . . but please let me explain.

"Today, walking back from my father's grave, I received a mobile phone call from my assistant at the Southwold Medical Clinic, where I care for many animals. Because I wanted and needed to be with my beloved father, and with family and friends, I had forgotten that I must . . . perform a very delicate surgery on a blind dog. This dog is named Farley. Farley was my father's favourite dog in the world. Pappino even tried to buy this dog, but his owners would not sell – at any price. So, whenever Pappino visited me, they would let him have Farley to play with. Pappino really loved that dog! And now Farley, this wonderful dog, is going blind. There is an operation that will let him see. It is a delicate and difficult operation. I have performed it before, and believe I can do it successfully for Farley. My father, before his last illness, had given Farley's owners money for this operation. It was important to my father, as it is to me, that Farley would see again. But, the longer I wait to perform the surgery, the harder it will be to save the dog's eyes. So . . . if you would let me go, a few days earlier than I should, I will be very grateful, as will Farley's owners, as will the poor dog. As, I believe, will be my father, who wanted so much for this operation to take place. So please, may I have your permission?"

Some were teary-eyed. Many were nodding. Phrases like *"poverettu cannuzzu"* could be heard, and, from my mother, *"Brava,* Ellissina! *La mia ragazzina ha un gran cuor!"* Family and friends all agreed that Ellissina, the little girl with the big heart, should be allowed to go home and save the blind dog.

That night, after being driven to Palermo, and then flying to Rome, Stellario and I flew to London. At Heathrow Airport, after clearing the customs queue, I rang Davy. It was a bit past midnight. "Sorry it's so late, love. Sicily was . . . well, it was a Sicilian funeral and in all the hullabaloo, there was no way to ring. I'm at the airport."

"Welcome home! How'd you bolt so soon? I thought Papp's pageant was to take weeks."

"It will take weeks. I managed to slip off early, with family consent. Listen, I really don't want to go to Papp's flat just now. Is it too late at night to come to you?"

"Of course not. It is, however, too late for coherent conversation. That needs to keep until the morrow. I'll make up your bed in the Ellissa Major Room."

"I'll try not to make noise coming in."

"Not to worry. I sleep in fancy French earplugs. As does Tariq."

At just past one in the morning. I sat in the back of a taxi, heading for Bayswater, eating rice balls from a slightly oily bag.

Stellario, saying goodbye at Heathrow terminal, kissed me on both cheeks and wished *"Tanti auguri* to the little blind dog. You will both be in my prayers." I didn't tell him that my father had not seen Farley for years, or that, if the dog had gone suddenly blind, I, his vet, knew nothing of it. As riddled with superstition as both my Sicilian parents, I clutched at the gold cross around my neck, the one I always wore to fly, and silently asked blessings for Farley's eyes.

DAVY AND TARIQ

The flat was freezing cold, due to my brother's life-long belief that circulating air from open windows, even the circulating air of central London in winter, was essential to health. Fortunately, he also believed in heavy duvets.

"Paid Screamers? Screamers as in people who scream or screamers as in Very Nelly Persons?"

"People who scream. Yer proverbial Little Old Ladies. Women from the town who are paid to scream at funerals."

Davy opened the kitchen window, breathed deeply and, delighted by a new espresso-toy, made two more cappuccinos.

"How much does it pay?"

"It looked more impressive in lire. Now it's forty Euros a day – about twenty-two quid."

"Not worth it. I'll keep my current gig."

"You're not a little old lady."

"For good money, I could be the best bloomin' little old lady you've ever seen, Madam."

He brought our coffees to the bright red kitchen table.

"Listen, Lissa, I didn't want to tell you last night . . ."

"Mareike changed the locks at Papp's flat?"

"How'd you know?"

"I know Mareike. 'Johnny Major's Legal Widow' was going to tighten the clamps on everything as fast as she could. How did *you* know? Did you go there?"

"Please don't look all worried. I wanted a particular thing . . . one of Papp's black cashmere cardigans. There was one on a chair in his bedroom. I tried it on. It was too big for me, but felt wonderful. So soft. And it smelled of him. I took it, and then worried that I shouldn't have. So, two nights ago, after Rupe the night porter would've gone off-duty, I went back to return it. I could open the entry door, the one used by everyone who lives in that block of flats, but when I got to Papp's, my key wouldn't work. There was a new second lock in the door as well. So I couldn't return the black cardie. I think it meant that I was meant to have it . . . I think . . ."

He put his hand over mine.

"I never asked for things from him, Lissa. Not once. He paid for my schooling, and anything else I needed as a child. Once I was grown, and earning money, it was just birthdays and Christmas. And a member of his staff usually selected those things. I gave him things all the time – little gifts I thought he'd enjoy. And he did enjoy them. Kept them on display in his flat or in his office. A music box that played *Nessun Dorma*, an ancient Roman bubble glass jar . . . I loved him, Lissa. And believe he loved me. He said he did, and he did not fling that sort of announcement about casually. I wanted . . . something of his . . ."

He was crying. I knelt on the floor and hugged him. "Go, Davy. Have your howl. I had mine in Sicily."

He cried for a while, for what had been, but also for what had not been. For that inhibiting clumsiness between men – even when they are father and son – even when the son is not gay and the father not overly involved with displaying various Butch Badges. I wanted to tell him about my dream/visit in Agrigento, but as with Mammina, something held me back. It wasn't the right time. I also needed to update him about what happened with Petra in New York. Again, it wasn't the time. Not during Davy's freedom to grieve, his howling time.

When Davy was fully wept out, I told him about the weeping wells. "When I was ten, and weeping over Helena's impending divorce from Papp, she said we all had wells of tears – weeping wells – and that it was sometimes good, *cleansing*, she said, to just weep until the well emptied. She said weeping wells always refilled, for the next time you need them."

"Weeping wells. I like that. That's me, Trelawney of the Weeping Wells."

"Who of the what?"

"*Trelawney of the Wells*. It's a 19th-century play. We did it at school. I was brilliant."

"I told everyone at the wake that you were a brilliant actor."

"You spoke about me at Papp's funeral?"

"Mm hm. Said you were making a telly film for children. Sicilians love children. They were very impressed. I told them you planned to visit Papp's grave as soon as you finish filming. Cousin Giuseppino will welcome you in his home. Pappino's first home, his father's as well."

"I always wanted to see Papp's childhood home. He kept saying he'd take me . . . but it didn't happen."

"Well, you'll see it soon. Have you ever met Cousin Giuseppino?"

"No. Except for Auntie Nan, I've never met any of the Maggiores. Papp's marriages and business things kept getting my Sicilian trip postponed. I never mentioned it. I thought he'd do it when he could. I never pushed it because I was afraid he didn't really want to. It would be funny if he thought I didn't want to . . ."

"Well, all the Maggiores are expecting you. Giuseppino is lovely. A softer, less competitive version of Pappino."

"A soft Johnny Major. I wonder what that would be like."

"Like you." His eyes filled but he grinned the Davy grin. "Of all the things you might've said, I like that one best."

"I'm glad. May I get off my knees now?"

"As the actress said to the Bishop."

"What?"

"Nothing. More theatre rubbish. So, you're not cross? About my taking one of Papp's cardies?"

"No, Davy, of course not. I'm glad you have it. Very glad, actually. But now I need to get back to Southwold. Check in with Betty and the assorted beasties. Sleep in my own bed. Try to figure out where we are and what . . ."

"There they are, Snow White and Rose Red. Good morning, you two."

Tariq stood in the kitchen archway – white YSL shirt, tailored slim jeans, sunlight bouncing off skin the colour of bleached terracotta. Davy swore that Tariq did nothing about looking perfect. Physically perfect, said Davy, was the state in which Tariq commenced and continued to be on earth.

Davy, seeing Tariq every day, had got used to The Face. I, on the other hand, was never quite ready for it: widely spaced black-brown eyes, film-star straight nose, prominent cheekbones, an almost rectangular smile, naturally perfect white teeth. And his hair. Midnight blue-black. Hanging, with a slight wave to just above his shoulders, the front falling into his eyes, affording him the opportunity, taken frequently, to head-toss it out of his line of vision.

Tariq knew he was good-looking. He was so very beautiful that not knowing would qualify him as an idiot. He didn't fuss with it much. Didn't have to. I don't think he knew how lucky I always felt when I got to look at him.

"Hello, *Bellissimo*."

He poured a black coffee and came to sit at the kitchen table, kissing the top of Davy's curly blond head, then tossing back his hair. "How was Sicily?"

"Very Sicilian. Beautiful and difficult . . . and a part of my heart."

"Did you learn anything more about the lost will?"

"No. It was neither the time nor the place. We'll be getting back on it now. These things are so bloody nasty when there's a lot of money involved."

"There doesn't have to be a lot of money involved, Ellissa. There can be next to nothing involved. Death turns even friends and family into vultures. When my mother died, we, all of us, haggled over bits of fabric, worn-out rugs, a few pieces of traditional jewellery. At a jumble sale, the lot would've brought about two hundred quid. And there we all were, pulling and tugging like . . ."

"Scavengers?"

"Exactly. And, on that cheery note, I have to go to a fabric shop in the East End and subtly match human attire to furniture. It's good to see you, Lissa. Will you be staying tonight?"

"Can't. Must get back to Southwold. Work awaits."

"Well, return to us soon. Let me fix us a Moroccan meal."

"Oh, yes. A definite yes." I stood and we hugged. Then I kissed his cheeks three times, right-left-right, as was his custom.

"I do like watching you and Davy together. You're like the blond and brunette of some ancient Janus. When you're together, you welcome me, but you do not need me. You are complete. Snow White and Rose Red. The . . . soul-weaving of blond and black-haired siblings. That story is where my nicknames for you two come from."

"I know. We read those stories constantly as kids. And who are *you*, Tariq?"

"Me? I'm Aladdin. And I must fly." And he was out the door.

Davy shook his head. "'Aladdin.' 'Must fly.' Dreadful. And my fault. I taught him punny word-games. Now I can't get him to stop!"

"What he said. About the two of us. It's exactly what you said, back in Montréal, about Pappino and me. Maybe it all really is like Noah's Ark. Humans are two-by-twos, in varying combinations at different times, with one or more others, however beloved, looking on."

Davy walked me to his door and onto the Bayswater Road. A cool sunny day. "So it's over? The missing will stays missing and Mareike wins the jackpot?"

"No. It isn't over. Somewhere in this world there is a document that would prove me to be a rightful heir. Which is not the point. It's not that I should have Papp's money; it's that all he built over years ending up as Mareike's surgery-and-wardrobe fund is obscene.

"My problem with defending Papp's will and wish is that wading into the slime-pit for a grudge-match with Mareike knocks me to the ground every time I think of it. Mareike's whole life has been about acquiring money. That sort of contest excites her. It sickens me. It would make our father's life be about his death, about his money. It wasn't and it isn't. I can't fight that fight."

"And I'd be . . . even less good at it than you. I'd probably bugger it up completely."

"You have great gifts, Bruvv, but yes, you'd probably bugger this up. Completely. Not to worry, though, I've turned the matter over to a true terrier, with a stronger talent for vengeance than either of us."

"Your mother."

"You've got it in one."

Intimate Strangers
in East Anglia

Being back in Southwold was like getting a vast orchestra of tambourines and cymbals to stop playing. I drank tea, joked with Betty and tended to the clinic's assorted critters. One had died of old age while I was gone.

"Farley?" I asked, trying to sound casual and businesslike.

"No. Joe Bloggs. Just died in his sleep"

"And Farley? Farley's well?"

"As far as I know, Ellissa. Quite old but fine. Why? Had he been ill before you left."

"No. He was . . . my father's favourite dog from the clinic, so he's just, been in my thoughts lately."

"I understand."

No, Betty. No, you don't, I thought. You are a bred-in-the-bone Englishwoman. You know nothing about the *malocchio*. Your employer, Doctor Major, just wanted to make sure she hadn't put a Sicilian curse on a sweet old East Anglian dog.

Dan and I resumed our sexual friendship. The local vet and the local chief police constable. Southwolders approved of this relationship, as it involved She Who Heals Animals and He Who Catches Villains. Some would drop brick-subtle hints about our eventually marrying. This was never going to happen, but it gave them gossipy pleasure to think it might. As for Dan and me, we were as we'd always been – two different species of animal who were at our best in bed. We had no clue, most times, what to talk about or how to say it in shared images, but the sweetness had remained. Actually, it intensified. Dan had not wished my father harm, but he was what Davy called a "three-b" – big, butch bloke – and, as such, seemed to feel bigger and stronger with his chief rival dead. His self-perceived new alpha status helped him to be consoling with me. One night, when I was trying to dream of Pappino and could not, I woke up and wept. He held me, murmuring, "I know, Liss. And I'm here."

No, you don't know, I thought. Not really. You'd have to have lived this thing to know. But I'm glad you're here.

I spoke with my mother infrequently, sometimes avoiding her calls. Mammina had a passion for murder mysteries, and became fond of saying things like "I've got a strong lead," "the trail's gone cold" and "I think we're closing in on 'em."

As with Davy, I'd never told Mammina what I'd discovered about Petra. If she knew that Petra had deliberately, and in league with Mareike, caused Pappino's death, she'd go after Petra. Mammina was a uni-focused hitwoman. A scent-based hunter. If she went after Petra, she would stop chasing the will. My father could not be brought back. The will could. There'd be time for discussing Petra, after we knew about the will.

WHERE THERE'S A WILL

Thanks to my mother the bollard (whom I'd re-christened my mother the bloodhound), we knew about the will two months after my father's funeral.

"Mauro Azzidone found it. It was in his cousin's office in Palermo. Mauro's cousin is a lawyer . . ."

"Mammina?"

"Please don't call me that. It makes Doug's kids feel left out . . ."

It was after midnight. Even with those I love, I am less patient after midnight. "Mammina! I am in my own house in England. In the middle of the night. None of Doug's kids are in this house. You are not calling yourself Mammina. I am calling you Mammina. In my own house. The one with none of Doug's kids in it, and . . ."

"Fine. Call me what you like. Do you want to know about your father's will?"

"His actual will?"

"Yes."

"You found his actual will?"

"You deaf? Yes, his actual will. Found it a month ago. In Palermo. There was no point saying anything until I knew it was solid. It's been thoroughly checked out by all sorts of top lawyers – Sicilian, Italian, English, and Canadian. It's solid."

I knew that one day a will would be found. Given Pappino's fiscal fastidiousness, it had to be. It was also true that, for my own sanity and sense of honour, I had been trying to let go of the whole money thing.

I'd wanted to keep our family money thing in the background since childhood. Every Friday at Peter Rabbit School had been a "wear what you wish, non-uniform day." We were instructed to "dress simply, and with one favourite thing, about which we would tell the class." I wore clean, pressed jeans and a long white shirt of my father's. The shirt had been made by Battistoni, in Rome, and had my father's monogram, *JPM*, on the right pocket. It was usually my sleep-shirt.

One of my classmates, Fliss, always wore somewhat shabby clothes. Even her everyday uniform looked frayed – I thought it might be a hand-me-down, as her elder sister, Dolly, had also attended the school. Fliss's favourite thing was a pair of multiply-darned socks, which she said had belonged to her grandmother. I worried that Fliss had no decent clothes, assuming that she was at school on a bursary, as was my friend Claire.

I told my father about this impoverished classmate. He asked her name. Fliss, Felicity Bretwode, I replied. Pappino informed me that Fliss's father was one of the richest men in England, and a Baronet. "The very rich are just cheap, that's all. We're lucky, Ellissina. We're not rich enough to be that cheap."

I laughed then, because my father did, but have always felt uncomfortable about unearned money, about the flaunting of wealth. I'd tried always to neither display nor discuss money; to share it, unfussily, with friends, family and the wider world.

With my father's death, and the highly suspect absence of his will, I had been made part of the greedyguts mud wrestle that had sometimes surrounded his life – more frequently his post-Mareike life, and most intensely since post-Mareike collided with post-mortem.

Having chosen to set my mother on the hunt, I knew I would have to receive and act upon what she found. If I didn't, my father, wherever he was, would be insulted that I was guilty about the fiscal aspects of his great success. And he would visit me every night for the rest of my life to call me a coward, a fool, and a disappointment.

Mammina, at the other end of the line, was rabbiting on. I'd been so much into my own thoughts that I'd heard nothing but sound.

Staring out the window towards the porch-lit Southwold Animal Clinic, I said, "Sorry, Mammina. I missed that last thing . . . There's a squirrel in the bird feeder and . . ."

"A squirrel in the bird feeder?! I'm talking to you about at least eighty million dollars and you got squirrels in your bird feeder? You got squirrels in your head!"

I laughed.

"You think this is funny?"

"No. I don't think it's funny. I think *I'm* funny. I think I'm ridiculous. No, not ridiculous. Frightened. I've always been . . . afraid of all this."

"I know that. Vanni knew that. I think that's a part of why he did what he did. It's in his letter. There is a formal will. A legal document. Detailed lawyer talk. He made it after his first heart attack. There's also a short letter from him, explaining everything in human language. You'll get a copy of the will, with all the 'whereas'-es and things. You'll also get a copy of his letter. You know there are going to be challenges, so . . . everyone who might be involved will receive copies. I can read the letter to you now. Should I?"

"Yes please," I whispered, unable to produce a full voice. I could hear Pappino telling me, when I had panic attacks as a child: "Breathe, Ellissina, breathe . . ."

Mammina began reading, in a precise, yet softer and gentler tone than her usual commanding staccato.

The letter was dated "1 November 2000, Palermo, Sicily." In essence, Pappino had, in the presence of prominent Italian and British barristers, left Mareike her Roman flat. Auntie Nan inherited her Montréal flat. She would continue to manage that building for as long as she wished to do so, with tenant-rental monies for her use re taxes and maintenance. After her death, I would inherit the building. Various items of Papp's clothing and sports equipment were left to Davy, Liddru, Cousin Giuseppino and Dr. Doug Robertson. His two race horses, Agrigento and Garibaldi, were left to Helena in Ireland.

There was a brief paragraph stating that, *My jewellery and those emergency monies that I have placed in a safe deposit box at my branch of Barclays Bank, London, shall, upon my death, be the property of Dr. Ellissa Giovanna Major and her brother, John David Major, to be divided equally between them.*

Then came the heart of the matter. Johnny Major – Giovanni Paolo Maggiore – had left the bulk of his considerable wealth to the teenaged children of Agrigento, to be administered by cousin Giuseppino and Ntoniu Paluzzi, Liddru's schoolteacher-son, and overseen by my mother and the senior Palermo barrister, *Dottore* Tullio Marcantonio. Upon Mammina's death, her administrative position would fall to me. If I were to pre-decease Mammina, eventually her administrative position would transfer to Davy. The funds were to be used for scholarships, which would *enable young Agrigentesi with specific dreams to turn those dreams into reality, as I have done.*

Papp went on to declare that *my daughter, Dr. Ellissa Giovanna Major and my son, Mr. John David Major, have successfully pursued their dreams. To now overwhelm them with money would suffocate their independence and curiosity, two traits I admire and love in them. It is nonetheless true that fortune is capricious. Should Dr. Ellissa Giovanna Major or Mr. John David Major, my sister, Mrs. Antoinetta (a.k.a Nanette) Muzzi or my first wife, now Mrs. Douglas Robertson of British Columbia, Canada, ever be in need of money for medical reasons, housing-related reasons, or in order to continue with their work, this money shall not be withheld. I trust each of them to deal honourably with this financial protection provision, as they always did while I lived.*

There was a paragraph about *fluctuating monies* from *various projects in which I am a partial investor and/or silent partner.* These items were listed and would also be monitored by the lawyers and my mother.

So. All the major Major monies and holdings had been left to the young people of Agrigento. I could not speak with absolute authority for Mr. John David Major, but, at that moment, Dr. Ellissa Major, Small Animal Veterinarian of Southwold, Suffolk, was astonished by, and grateful to my fierce self-made Southern Italian father who was wise in everything except some sexual partnering choices. And that was, to paraphrase my mother, because men sometimes followed their dicks into blonde alleys filled with brigands. Tears of relief rolling out of my eyes, I started to laugh uncontrollably.

"Ellissina? You all right? You all right with this? Ellissina?"

"Oh, Mamma," I replied breathlessly, "I am *very* all right with this! It is . . . all so completely right. He knew. He knew I did not want to be a casino-owning millionairess. We are all right and . . ."

"The Dutch bitch is all wrong!"

"Uh . . . right."

The last paragraph of the letter stated that *In placing initial co-administration with Mrs. Ellissa Robertson, I am in no way questioning the fiscal competence, worth or rights of my daughter, Dr. Ellissa Giovanna Major, who has been a continuing joy to me during my lifetime. I simply believe that she will need some time and distance to fully accept the fact of my death.*

Breathe, Ellissina, breathe.

There was so much information to take on board. And that was just the summarising letter. My fingers tingled and I kept gulping.

"'The emergency monies.' Some things never change."

"What?"

"Vanni's emergency monies in Barclays Bank. He needed 'emergency monies' like I need two heads. But if you're born without much money you always think it could all disappear."

"It almost did."

"Yeah.You know, there was more money and watches and stuff under a loose floorboard, under our bed in the Montréal apartment too. After he died, I told Nanette to check. It was still there. I told her to keep it. Is that OK?"

"What?"

"Do you want your Aunt Nanette to give that money and jewellery to you and your brother, or is that not the same, being in Montréal and . . ."

"Mammina, it's fine. Auntie Nan is welcome to those things. We don't have to . . . to litigate the board under the bed in Montréal. We – you, me and Davy – we don't have to litigate anything."

"So you're OK with waiting for me to die before you administrate?"

I wanted to shout. At Peter Rabbit School, in Deportment class, Mrs. Dearing always said, "When you wish to shout, instead, remember to make your voice as soft and clear as possible. It is far more commanding of attention. It is also gracious behaviour, which shouting is not." (Mrs. Dearing, to my knowledge, had no Southern Italian roots.) "Mammina, I am not 'waiting for you to die.' I do not wait for people to die."

The times when my mother permitted herself to sound embarrassed and flustered in public could be counted on the fingers of one hand, with the thumb left over. This conversation used up the thumb. "No, no, Ellissina . . . I didn't mean you were waiting for me to die. I only meant . . ."

"I know what you meant, it's all right. Look, I need a bit of time. Just an hour. To . . . absorb all this. Will you be home in an hour? May I ring you back?"

"Sure. I'll wait for your call. Ellissina?"

"Yes."

"I love you."

"Me too you."

"'Me too you.' You got that from your father. Hedging his bets. I want the whole thing, the whole fucking out-loud thing."

"I love you, Mammina."

"Good. Call me in an hour."

FULLY COMFORTED,
FULLY PISSED,
TOTALLY TERRIFIED

I walked downstairs from my bedroom to the parlour and sat for a while in the dark. I rarely drink, and never drink much, so it was somewhat impressive that I found the bottle of Grappa in the dark and more impressive that I drank two water tumblers of it.

Finding my father's will was meant to happen. It was a just and good thing.

That comforted me. Or I knew it should.

Knowing it should comfort me comforted me.

My lumpily overstuffed brown velour armchair comforted me.

My legs, pulled up into a half-lotus position comforted me.

The ticking of the cuckoo clock comforted me.

The darkness comforted me.

A stomach-warming bucket's worth of Grappa comforted me.

Everything else that had became fully activated in my life with one phone call from my mother – those things, and all things that might metastasise from those things totally terrified me. Though Mammina and I said nothing about it, we both knew that Mareike, the Greedhead from Hell, would challenge the found will. There would be a period (I'd no idea how long) of bad people behaving badly and not-so-bad people behaving fiercely. I would be part of all this bad behaviour and fierceness.

Or I could change my name and move to the beautiful island of Brac. In the former Yugoslavia. Nobody knew I knew anyone on the beautiful island of Brac, in the former Yugoslavia. They would never

think to look for me there. I could come back later, when the gladia-
torial carnage in the law courts was over and only my mother or
Mareike was still standing, covered in gore, covered in glory, covered
in money, covered in all of the appropriate documents and deeds.

The cuckoo clock said it was past two in the morning. The phone
rang.

"Ellissina? Are you all right?"

"A bit drunk, Mammina, a bit shaky. Otherwise fine."

"The lawyers notified the Dutch bitch. I never knew they could do
that in the middle of the night. There will be a 'legal proceeding' with
English legal people deciding about Vanni's missing will and our challenge. The Dutch bitch knows Feinblatt's a problem, so she's retained
a Queen's Counsel expensive lawyer – the rumour is she used to be his
girlfriend. She used to be so many people's girlfriend that I'm amazed
she isn't bowlegged. Or bowmouthed. I'm going to kill her. She has no
right to try and take what's not hers, her and that Feinblatt who I
never trusted. His father, yes, him no. He's weak, Feinblatt, the son.
Another jerk always following his dick. So, like you said, Feinblatt did
a deal with the Dutch bitch and got his divorce money. The *stronza*
thought she could have everything, so now she gets nothing."

"She gets what she's already spent. And her flat in Rome. Papp
wanted her to have that."

"Not if she goes down. Not if she's inside. I'm going to sue her for
trying to hide Vanni's will. There are legal names for what she did.
They're criminal acts. They'll send her to jail. She can't do jail time.
She's a hundred years old. It'll kill her."

"I'm going now, Mammina."

"Going?"

"To the beautiful island of Brac."

"*Where?*"

"The beautiful island of Brac. It's spelt B-r-a-c, but it's pronounced
'Bratch.'"

"Where the hell is that?"

"In the former Yugoslavia."

"You're going to Yugoslavia?"

"No. I'm going to bed. I'll talk to you in the morning."

If you're not much of a drinker, and you've just gulped down three full tumblers of very strong Italian alcoholic bev, closing your eyes is not an option. The room goes round and round. If you keep your eyes open, the room does not go round and round, but the way you feel transcends "wonky" and enters the zone of "Feel like I'm gonna die . . . and I certainly hope so."

My old oak four-poster bed, pride of a Felixstowe flea market, was too high off the ground for me to step from bed to floor while in Grappa-driven disrepair. So I did it like a large arthritic dog: slowly put my front paws to the mustard-coloured sisal carpet, then dragged my back paws along behind. Knocking me to the ground, on my right buttock cheek. I crawled to the loo, lifted the toilet seat and, sitting on the cool black and white tile floor (to avoid pitching forward and drowning head-first), chundered until I was a clean vessel. I said it aloud – "clean vessel," nodding with satisfaction. I stretched out on my side, pressing my right facecheek to the cool tile, then rolled onto my back and lay there for a while.

Goran. Did Goran still have that cottage on the island of Brac? Was he still painting? Were his paintings any better? Would he want to paint the fifty-year-old me? He wanted to paint the twenty-five-year old me. He wanted to fuck the twenty-five-year old me. He did both. The fucking was better than the paintings, though he took both very seriously.

Crikey, I thought, you, *Dottore* Major, are totally pissed. Old Goran likely has a Mrs. Goran by now. And three or four little Goranettes and Goranumpuses. Goranumpus? What is the male for Goran? Oh Ellissa, you pissed twit, the male for Goran is Goran.

I sat up, steadying myself with my hands, letting my head drop to my chest. "Oh good," I said, "no meningitis." If you can lower your head to your chest, you do not have meningitis. I learned that when Sal's brother Marcello got meningitis in Capri, some twenty years earlier. From that day forward I would periodically lower my head to my chest, gratefully announcing "Oh good. No meningitis."

Meningitis-free yet again, I slowly stood up and, steadying myself on various walls, doors and articles of furniture, clambered onto the four-poster. I lay on my side, eyes ready for closing without room-spinnage, and sank quickly into dreamless sleep.

MAREIKE DOES MEDIA

Within days, "Major Will War" (as one headline read) was all over the papers. Well, perhaps not "all over" the papers, given the front-page status of escalating world lunacies, ecclesiastical paedophilia, inter-ethnic discord, plus the bed arrangements and public perform-ance exhibitions of half-naked celebrities with tiny bodies and enor-mous breasts. If, however, you were a member of the extended or distended Major family, a friend/enemy to any of the key players or just a lover of sleaze and dish, the relevant items could be found in the pages of newspapers and magazines, on radio and on telly. Information was also available on the Internet if you typed in John Major, Mareike DeLyn, John David Major, Ellissa Robertson or Ellissa Major.

Mareike, seeing an opportunity to appear in public as the world's oldest Hot Chick, held a press conference in Pappino's London flat. The press corps (including Tariq, who'd borrowed an accreditation card from a friend who worked at the magazine *Morocco in London*) was served tea, coffee, mineral waters and biscuits.

After about fifteen minutes, Mareike descended the stairs, slowly enough for everyone to see her before she reached the bottom step. She wore a dove-grey sheath suit, cream-coloured sling-back low-heeled pumps and a silk blouse of the same colour. The blouse had a rounded Peter Pan collar; a style, according to Davy, "frequently favoured by women who murder their aged husbands . . . but not usually favoured by aged women." The wig was new to me – the Hamlet pageboy style, but in a darker blonde, intermingled with shiny strands of either light brown or almost white blonde. Her thick tousled fringe usually meant a forehead facepeel would soon follow, unless, finally, she had so little forehead skin left that one more peel would hit bone.

She circulated among the media types, smiling and thanking, then crossed the room to Pappino's old wine-red leather chair, which, as always, was placed at an angle to my child-sized wine red chair. On my chair was a huge bulbous vase filled with lilies.

"Fuckin' 'ell!" I shouted at the screen. "Get that bloody . . ."

"Prop," Davy offered.

"Prop. Get that bloody prop off my chair, you old ghoul!"

"The flowers are small beer, Lissa. Look behind her!"

Above the mantle, where Pappino had, for years, hung a rather expensive Scottish oil of two horses frolicking in a field, was an enormous painting of John Major, at about age seventy-five (by which time they had long since separated, and rarely spoke unless money was involved). He stood in front of a red velvet curtain. Seated next to him, face in three-quarter profile gazing up adoringly, was Mareike, looking about twenty-eight. Both painting and press conference featured the same dove-grey suit and Peter Pan collared blouse. Somebody's hair was atop her head and pulled into a low ponytail. The painting was the world's largest piece of romance novel cover art. Davy said he'd not seen it on his recent trip to Papp's ("And I would have noticed a monstrosity of such size and uglitude!").

"She must have commissioned it for the press conference."

"She probably sold the painting of the horses. I loved that painting."

Seating herself in Papp's chair, Mareike crossed her legs, angling both feet slightly to the right. She then opened a pale grey folded paper and looked out through her uncloseable wide eyes. She was sitting at the same three-quarter angle as in the huge painting – an angle I'd once heard her describe as "best for showing my cheekbones." Her voice sounded small and soft – young but not girlish. I'd never heard this voice before. The accent was more Brit than Dutch. It was usually more French than Dutch.

"Thank you all for being here. This is . . . a difficult and embarrassing time for me, as I know it would be for my late husband, were he still alive."

Mammina, amazingly silent to this point, whisper-hissed, "Your late husband, *buttana*, were he still alive, would kick your ass until it broke!"

"What's a *buttana*?" Davy whispered in my ear

"Whore," I mouthed in response.

"Thought so," Davy whispered, smiling. "I am half Italian, you know."

"Ssh," Mammina said. "Garbage is speaking."

Mareike sighed. Her considerable chest heaved. Cameras whirred and clicked. "As most of you know, John and I did not live together conventionally. He could have divorced me at any time, but chose not to. It was John's way of saying 'I love you.' It was 'John's way of saying he didn't want to marry anyone else ever again."

Mammina started making retching gagging noises, pointing her index finger into her mouth. I glared at her. She stopped, settling for biting down hard on the finger. "A stupid vain mistake! Until the day he died, Vanni thought he was this big stud who needed . . ."

"Ssh, Mammina. We must listen. Garbage is speaking."

In her new voice, with a lineless but limited range of facial expressions, Mareike continued: "When John died, I became responsible, as his legal widow, for his considerable estate. It was my intention, and that of our two daughters, Floris and Petra, to establish charities and cultural endowments in his name. Shortly before he died, he told me what he wished to have done, as I sat beside his bed in a Canadian hospital. Everything was proceeding as it should, with respect for the dead and hope for the living. And then, from out of nowhere comes this woman who he married when they were both so young . . ."

"Young! He was thirty-fucking-eight years old, you lying whore!"

"*Dzito*, Mammina!" I shouted. "You can fight her later. We need to hear her now. Please."

"You're right, Ellissina. She makes me crazy, but now we listen."

"This Missus Robertson, the first of five wives, a woman who has had another husband for many years, and who did not even speak to John until he was on his deathbed, this Missus Robertson suddenly appears. In probable collusion with her daughter and another of John's children . . ."

"John David! My name is John David, you ditz! She doesn't even know my name! Mind you, neither did my father, most days . . ."

". . . This Missus Robertson has somehow created a fantasy will, naming an Italian village as the beneficiary of all that John had worked so hard for all his life, with her, this Missus Robertson from Canada, as an administrator of these monies, which will go God knows where. I am legally advised not to speculate on where sums of money may go, so I will not.

"The point is that John, starting as a poor immigrant but ending as an international success, has contributed handsomely to the wealth of at least four countries. A tradition that our two daughters and I would certainly continue, in all the countries now benefiting from my late husband's generosity. But this Missus Robertson, this other man's wife from Canada, this almost-stranger, with her self-serving phoney invented will, is trying to put herself in control of my beloved late husband's estate. Both for our twin daughters and for the cultural and charitable good of the United Kingdom, Canada, Italy and the Netherlands, I will use all legal means to fight this challenge to my rightful standing as executrix of my late husband's will. I will expose this will as the fraudulate thing it is."

Marieke smiled, refolded her paper, thanked everyone again, and posed for pictures under the grotesque painting and alongside the carved oak railing leading up the spiral steps. She then waved, a small royal-papal variant, and slowly ascended the stairs. As the press ran from the room to put their stories out in the world, I heard someone whisper "nice ass."

"Padded knickers," I muttered. "She's been flat-arsed for years."

"Fraudulate?" Davy wondered.

"English isn't her first language. She doesn't really think in English."

"If she thinks any of her lying shit is going to prevail in court, Ellissina," Mammina shouted, "she doesn't think in any language. *La guerra commincare!*"

The battle had begun.

A MAJOR MUD-WRESTLE

Throughout Marieke's will challenge there were telephone calls, doorstep arrivals and e-mails from media people. To one and all, I replied: "This is an ongoing legal process. I cannot discuss it. My love for and trust in my late father, my mother and my brother, John David Major is absolute and unwavering. I look forward to a swift and just resolution of this matter."

I was interviewed by a panel of judges and required to submit a written document detailing conversations with my father, Mareike, Davy and, most particularly, Eddie Feinblatt, re my father's will. I was also asked to write about Petra Major, my father's death, Petra's forgeries and our subsequent conversation in New York. As most of these conversations were without third-party witnesses, they could not stand alone as evidence but contributed to an understanding of what one of our lawyers called "patterns of malevolent intent by Mrs. Mareike DeLyn Major."

Petra had also been summoned to the proceedings to give testimony, but could not be found.

Dr. Marc Belliveau of Hôpitale Ste. Bernadette de Montréal could be found. He flew to England and gave oral and written testimony concerning Mareike's bizarre behaviour with my father's life support tubes.

Mammina also believed that Mrs. Major and Mr. Edward Feinblatt did not know, when destroying earlier wills, that a fully vetted later last will and testament existed in Palermo (referred to in the tabloids as either "The Sicilian Will" or, if that was too subtle, "The Sicilian Will of Cognoscenti Casino's Godfather").

In the end, given the mountain of international legal affirmation, corroborative depositions and statements, the Palermo will was declared to be my father's authentic last will and testament. Mammina was declared executrix. Mareike, in collusion with Eddie Feinblatt, was charged with criminally destroying legal documents for personal gain. Further it was decreed, in various countries and languages, that the Sicilian will was to be put into effect *ab initio* (legalese for immediately). Eddie Feinblatt would be investigated in Canada, and could be disbarred.

Our side's case had turned out to be so solid that the entire soap opera took only three weeks (not counting Mammina's ongoing lawsuit plans, which Davy said "might make the Hundred Years' War look like a coffee-break").

MAMMINA DOES MEDIA,
PETVET DOES ANIMAL RITES

Mammina held a press conference at her rented London flat. She said she always knew the truth would prevail because "there was no way this couldn't happen." She declared her intention to sue Mrs. Mareike DeLyn Major for various and sundry acts of "dishonourable disgrace" that ignored the last wishes of John P. Major. These wishes were known to her, and to Mr. Edward G. Feinblatt, barrister and solicitor, through documents from the late John Major, which had been in Mr. Feinblatt's possession, until he, Mr. Feinblatt, at the request of Mrs. DeLyn Major, destroyed said documents.

She announced her intention to sue Mrs. Mareike DeLyn Major and Mr. Edward Feinblatt for recovery of five million dollars, Canadian, which belonged to John Major, and were paid to Mr. Feinblatt in exchange for Mr. Feinblatt's destroying the earlier wills. The illegally destroyed wills named the same beneficiaries that were named in the Sicilian will. Said five million dollars had been paid to Mrs. Rachel Feinblatt, now the ex-wife of Mr. Feinblatt, for divorce costs, maintenance of her "standard of living," as well as tuition and related expenses of Jason Feinblatt, minor son of Edward and Rachel Feinblatt.

Further, she intended to sue Mrs. Mareike DeLyn Major, in Canada, for the attempted murder, in hospital, of Mr. John Major, and for colluding with Miss Petra Major in causing the death of Mr. John Major at the Ste. Bernadette Recuperation Centre.

Mammina's public style, a unique combination of working-class lawyer, Humphrey Bogart and the world's tiniest female hitperson, became a source of interest, amusement and, for a brief period, media parody.

During this time, when not writing depositions or in court, I focused on my veterinary tasks, which included:

Removing cataracts from the eyes of three cats.

Euthanising a cancer-riddled sixteen-year-old Golden Retriever.

Attending the funeral of an Irish Wolfhound who'd had a heart attack.

Tending to a litter of Sheepdog puppies.

Brushing and scaling twenty sets of dog teeth (except for Asterix, an Alsatian with tooth-gunk so thick that surgery was required).

Splinting the leg of a tire-biting spaniel.

Fitting a pelvic truss for Coco, a beagle suffering with Hound Ataxia, which caused his deteriorating and misaligned pelvis to swing from side to side whenever he tried to walk forward.

Almost everything else at the clinic was done by Betty, who understood that I had missed my animal-centred life, but also knew my focus was somewhat divided.

I wanted the comfort of Dan's big male presence, but there were too many tabloidoids in the bushes for the region's Chief Constable to be seen anywhere near me. We did manage two nights in a small hotel in Cuckold's Green, chosen because its name had always made us laugh (and because it was easy driving distance from Southwold, but far enough away from the "curtain-twitchers"). This brief getaway involved two cars, skulking off in the dead of night and too much paranoid dissembling for my overloaded brain and psyche. Dan and I agreed to take a holiday somewhere in the sun when the madness subsided.

Mammina and Malocchio

As threatened, Mammina commenced launching a paper armada of lawsuits against Mareike and Eddie Feinblatt, individually and collectively.

"She asked to stay in Vanni's flat for two weeks more. She said she needed time to move her personal things back to Rome. I said sure. I figured 'Go ahead, have time. Have time before you do time.' I went in there yesterday, with a lawyer and your brother. We inventoried everything and removed most of Vanni's things, except furniture. The stuff's in a secure storage vault. We'll get it once the *stronza* is back in Rome."

"My little red leather armchair is still at Pappino's?"

"Yeah. With the other furniture."

"I'd feel better if it were out of there."

"I'll get it tomorrow and bring it when I come to see you next week."

"Too much work. Let Davy hold it at his place."

"Okay. I'll call him and make arrangements. You know, Ellissina . . ."

The pause was so long that I thought we'd been disconnected. "Mammina?"

"Yeah. I'm here. I was just thinking, we did good. We won our case. We did right for your father – and for ourselves if we're being honest. But, dammit, when I think of what she is, and the things she's done, I just want her punished. Nah, truth is, and I don't like this about myself, but truth is I want her dead. I don't want that on my head though. I mean I wish . . . I wish she'd just die, without my doing anything."

"Marunkle's dead." It was five in the morning. "What? Davy? That you?"

"Yeh. Mareike's dead. It's all over the papers. Died yesterday at about this time, no, earlier . . . it says 'Time of death is approximated as four yesterday morning.' She fell down the stairs at Papp's flat. They didn't find the body until last night at eight when a Hungarian producer, that's what it says, 'Gabor Zsabo, Hungarian film producer,' came to take Mareike to dinner. Old Rupe the porter couldn't rouse anyone. So he went upstairs, heard Floris weeping, opened the door, and there was Marunkle with Floris kneeling over her body. It says that when Floris saw Rupe and the Hungarian, she started to scream. The police came. A paramedic gave Floris a tranquillizer and she was taken to a copshop to be interviewed. There's a full colour picture of Marunkle, face down in her dressing gown – excuse the rhyme – and all crumply at the bottom of the stairs. She's just about bald. Sort of baby-chick fluff on her scalp. One of the 'bloids, in its unwavering good taste, has a photo of her egghead in E.C.U . . ."

"E.C.U.?"

"Extreme close-up. She has a lovely head shape, actually. There's also a larger shot. That new pageboy wig, the one with the highlights and lowlights, is lying half under her face. Must've come off when she fell. Florid is crouching next to her and her eyes are huge and . . ."

"She has three fingers of her right hand curled over her upper lip."

"Exactly. How'd you know that?"

"It's what she does when she's in trouble. She does that and sometimes also hits her mouth and says 'Bad Floris.' Did she kill Mareike?"

"Dunno. Story says Mareike was in high-heeled shoes and may've slipped and fallen down the stairs. It says Floris was weeping and screaming and kept repeating 'She fell. Mama just fell.' It says the police are investigating further. Listen, Lissa, I have to go to the *Jimmy JollyJumper* studio immediately. I can drive out to you tonight, and leave at four-ish in the morning. Filming again tomorrow."

"Thanks for the offer, but that's a zoo for you. I'm coming to London on Sunday. Now, I'll go find a paper. Thanks for . . . sparing me the shock."

It was front-page in the tabs and second or third page in the broadsheets. Some papers did columns about Johnny's life and/or our recent kerfuffle re his will. Mr. Kingsmill, our local newsagent, who'd followed the will saga, as had all of Southwold, was doing a dreadful job of pretending I wasn't in the news (He's a sweet old gent, and the owner of a terrier called Robbie). To save us both embarrassment, I gathered and paid for five different papers without looking at them and drove back to the Animal Clinic. Betty already knew the situation and said she'd "hold the fort" while I read the papers in my office.

One article said that when Mareike fell she must have spilled the contents of an opened jar of acidophilus. The police identified the acidophilus when they tested the contents of the capsules, which were described as "an initially suspicious white powder." I knew acidophilus as the bacteria found in yoghurt. Why didn't Mareike just eat yoghurt? Perhaps, I thought, she had lactose intolerance.

The pageboy wig, as Davy had said, fanned out from underneath her face. She'd landed face down. I wondered if her eyes were open, wondered whether she'd been fully made up. I'd never seen her otherwise. Papp had once told me that she went to bed in a light makeup, in case she died in her sleep.

I knew that Mammina, in true Sicilian fashion, would believe she'd caused Mareike's death by wishing she'd "just die." I rang her. The line was engaged. That was because she was trying to ring me. Five minutes later Betty stuck her head in the door and said, "Yer Mum's on the phone."

"I killed her."

"No you didn't. And don't say that to anyone else; there are damn few Sicilians attached to the London constabulary."

"But I said . . ."

"That you wished she'd just die without your having to do anything. Repeat. *Without your having to do anything.*"

"But I did say . . ."

"Mammina . . . you are a . . . very strong person . . . but you can't will people dead by wishing they'd die."

"My mother could. Her mother could. One time . . ."

"Mammina, I can't do this now. Mareike's death has absolutely nothing to do with you. What *does* have to do with you, with all of us, is whether this death, which has nothing to do with you, puts paid to the need to sue anyone for anything. That would be lovely. It would mean that we could all get out of battle mode and back to living our lives."

"Not quite. I'm still suing Feinblatt."

"Ah yes. Right."

"And, if you wanted to, Ellissina, there is a case to be made against the skinny Dutch daughter. For pretending to be you, for forging your name, for taking Vanni to that place, which hastened his death. That's the word the lawyer used, 'hastened.' That's really your case, not mine. It's about you. About you and Vanni and the skinny Dutch. I know you liked her, but she still . . ."

The boulder that had so recently rolled off the top of my head rolled back to its former location. I sighed.

"You don't have to, if you don't want to. But Marcantonio says you have a case."

"I know. Let me think about that. And let me know where the lawyers say Mareike's death places things. It's all a bit . . . grim and strange. I'm weary of it. All of it."

"It should be over very soon. No more than six months or a year."

"A year?"

"Feinblatt. And . . . maybe the Dutch twins."

"Right. Thanks for ringing. I'll talk to you later."

I buzzed Betty on the phone for a cup of tea.

"Coming up. And Makedda's had her litter. We've seven new Abyssinian kittens in the surgery."

"Brilliant. I'll drink my tea and then have a look at the Makedda-Babies."

Teacup in hand, I walked over to my office window. A grey day. I could feel my father near. Looked up. Saw nothing but lowering clouds and a black bird. "Oh, Pappino mio, are you trying to reach me but having red tape? Do you know Mareike is dead? If you do and you're sad about it, I offer my sympathy. I know you cared for her once. Maybe you never fully stopped caring. I didn't want her to die. I just wanted her . . . not in our lives. When you died, I wanted to find your will. And we did. Please come see me if you can. In the mean-time I do hope you're still flying about in soft weather, barefoot and half erect, with no grudges to settle . . . and doing well in your sculpture class."

Dan had been ringing me, on both my mobile and the phone at my place. He'd also come to the clinic. I asked Betty to tell him I'd get back to him. I knew he'd want to help, want to console. And that I'd hate it, feel crowded by it. This was family business and he was *straniero*, a stranger.

My mobile phone played the Albinoni *Adagio*. Caller I.D. read "Davy."

"Hullo, Bruvv. Glad you rang. I've a question."

"About what?"

"Acidophilus. Why do you think Mareike had a jarful of aci-dophilus when she . . . fell or was pushed?"

"Don't you know about acidophilus?"

"It's the bacteria in yoghurt."

"Mm hmm. It's also a lubricant."

"Acidophilus?"

"Yes. A non-chemical natural shover-upper."

"Oh yuck. Do I want to know this?"

"You're fifty years old. Yes you do. For future reference."

"Well, that's charming and cheering. Do go on."

"You shove the capsule up . . . your orifice of choice, the gelatine dissolves and the acidophilus becomes a slightly sticky white goo. Without the chemical smell or side effects."

"I'll be damned."

"Probably not. But you will be dry. Eventually. Marunkle was some amazing age and, without lubricant, a veritable Sahara, I'm sure."

"She did expect this Hungarian producer, for whom she may've wished to be . . ."

"Moist."

"Right."

"He couldn't be involved in her death. Rupe let him in, a fair while after she . . . Lissa, before, you said 'fell or was pushed.' Which do you think – 'fell' or 'pushed?'"

"Neither. There's more news in the afternoon papers. She'd been really bunged up. Davy, I think she was thrown. Very hard. After being killed. No matter what her age, too many bones were broken for just a fall, or even a push. Her face was smashed in. She'd spent so much money, over the years, on that face. Even in a fall, she would've tried to protect it. I don't *know* that she was thrown. Or killed first. But it's what I think."

"That's so violent. So . . . Sicilian."

"And *that* is offensive."

"Is it wrong?"

"Not necessarily, but it *is* offensive."

"And the only Sicilian with access to the newest set of locks is . . ."

"My mother."

"Crikey. Do you think . . . ?"

"No I don't. Mareike was definitely not moisturising for my mother. And Mammina would only try to do her in with *malocchio*."

"What's that when it's at home?"

"The evil eye."

MURDER IS THE THING
WITH FEATHERS

Papp's flat had been designated "the scene of an ongoing criminal investigation" but my mother, as legal owner of the property, could come and go, as long as she took a police constable with her.

She found the bird.

Three days after Mareike's death, they were, according to the newspapers, up in Pappino's bedroom, which Mareike had been using. She had filled two refrigerator-sized boxes with Papp's clothes and stocked his dressing room with some of her own massive wardrobe. Mammina, in gloves given her by the constable, with him watching her, was searching through the clothes, looking for anything of Papp's, Davy's or mine that Mareike might've taken.

The bird, a crow, lay in the top drawer of a small cosmetics-filled wooden chest. Papp had kept photographs of his wives and children in that chest. The photos were gone. The crow had glossy red lipstick smeared all over its orange beak. The two halves of the beak had been pried open and stuffed with a hand-carved miniature wooden penis, complete with perfectly spherical testicles that were pushed up onto each side of the broken beak, securing the penis in place. The bird's black feathers were streaked with blond dye. Its neck and legs were broken. A pale pink felt-tip marker protruded from its cloacal orifice. And, according to the papers, it 'reeked of perfume.' Mammina identified the scent as *Acqua di Parma*. She told the constable that it was the cologne my father had worn. "The same one as Cary Grant," the paper quoted her as saying.

The police dusted the wooden chest. No fingerprints. I didn't need fingerprints to know who'd killed and decorated the bird. Had she also killed her mother? Floris seemed to be a witness to her mother's death. Where was Floris?

I knew I should ring the police. I rang my mother. She wasn't home. Where was she? Had she seen the newspapers? She'd read my written statements. She, finally, knew about Petra and Papp. Davy knew about Petra and birds. Had either of them shared any of this with the police? Our will-related statements were mostly still private. Had the police who found the decorated and violated dead crow seen our statements? If so, why had they not contacted me? Or Mammina? Or Davy? Davy was on the *Jimmy JollyJumper* set without a newspaper in sight. Happily singing, tumbling and clapping his gloved hands in Kiddie Telly Land while a deeply wounded homicidal woman was somewhere in London, along with the family members she might most want to kill. Except her half-sister, who was in Southwold trying to immediately alert the rest of that family.

I tried Davy's mobile. Even though he'd be working, leaving a text message felt better than doing nothing. What sort of message, I wondered as I jabbed at the tiny number-pad? Your skinny Dutch half-sister is on the loose in London and may be killing people and birds? Decided that wouldn't do. Left no message, but decided to go immediately to London.

I still hadn't rung the police. Right, I thought. I would ring the police. In the tradition of my people, I rang *my* police.

"Dan. It's Liss."

"Liss. I've been . . . following everything in the papers and on telly. I've telephoned a few times. Also stopped at both the clinic and the house, spoke to Betty, asked her to ask you . . ."

"I know."

"I've been worried about you."

Oh God, I thought, don't guilt me now, Dan, there's no time. I need you. In your official capacity. "I know, Dan. And I'm . . . very grateful. It was all so sudden and so creepy. I had to be quiet and alone for a bit. We do have an emergency though. I want to ask your help."

I told him as much as possible, as fast as possible. He was at my place fifteen minutes later.

With a detachable blue police-light rotating atop Dan's grey Volvo, we were in London in what had to be record time and had parked in front of the BBC building in Wood Lane. A uniformed guard at the information desk said the cast was just beginning afternoon tea break and that Mr. John David Major was in his dressing room. He said he had to ring before letting me go up. He said, "'E's 'avin' a right fam'ly reunion, innee? 'Is sister Ellissa is up wiv 'im naow." He smiled broadly. "An' which sister are you, ven?"

"Petra. I'm his sister Petra. And this gentleman is Mister Dan McCabe, a friend of ours from Southwold."

The guard rang Davy's dressing room. "You got anuvver sister 'ere, Mister Major. Missus Petra Major's 'ere, wiv a Mister McCabe from Soufwold, an' 'ey'd like to come up t'see you." He passed the phone to me.

"Hello, Davy. It's me. Sister Petra. Is . . . our other sister with you?"

"Oh . . . yes. Petra is here. She's brought me a beautiful bird, in an antique Victorian cage. A Cockatiel, she says it is. With a plume atop its head. Like my gelled hair. And round red Jimmy JollyJumper cheek-feathers. Very flash. And you can teach it to speak. I told her I'd train it to cue me when I'm learning lines. We're having tea and sarnies and . . . getting acquainted."

"Davy. We've bought the rights to that old horror film again. The Montréal . . . name-exchange thing. My visit should be a reunion surprise. Don't tell Sis. I'm coming up now. Me, Petra. OK?"

"Yes. Sure. Brilliant."

"Keep your eyes on her at all times . . . You know how she loves your big brown eyes. At all times. I'm coming up now. Keep smiling, stay charming."

"Will do."

"Great. May Dan McCabe, my friend from East Anglia, come up with me? He'll wait just outside the door while we have our family reunion and then join us when we're ready. "

"That's Dan deBillo?"

"Right. Chief Constable Dan. I'll pass the phone to the security officer now."

The guard listened to Davy for a moment, said 'very good, sir,' then looked up at Dan and me. "You can bofe go on up, Missus. Ayf floor. Turn right when you get out uvva lift. Dressing room one. Mister Major's name is on vuh door."

Waiting for the lift, everything felt scary, tentative and delicate. What I needed, what I wanted to hear, was my father. In the sound-lines between us was a large man. The large man was not happy with what I'd arranged.

"Look, Liss, this sounds like a very sick woman. A woman who may have already murdered at least once. I think we should go in together . . . as a couple. No police. Just a man and woman."

"Dan. I've no idea . . . how this is going to go. I do know that Petra is both fierce and fragile. No matter how angry she is at me, at all the Majors, I believe she still wants me as a sister. We had a fairly cold discussion in New York, about her role in our father's death. She wanted sisterhood and I shut her out. I need to try reaching out for her now. If I don't, I believe Davy is in danger."

"What about you, Liss? Aren't you in danger?"

"Probably. But she seems to have an order for these things. If I were 'next' in her plan, she'd've come out to Southwold. She didn't. She's here. With Davy. She brought him a bird. I think I see what's happening. And she is family. I have to play my hunch, and I have to play it, at least at the start, alone. If she sees a stranger, she could get . . . very squirrelly, very crazy." The lift came. We entered and the doors shut. "Look, let me get into Davy's dressing room, and then you move, very quietly, to outside his door. If it all goes bazonkers, I'll call your name . . . and in you come. I believe we must do it this way. Please."

"It makes me, as you say, 'squirrelly' . . . but you know her. You know your brother. I'll try it outside the door. I will be listening, and if I think you're in danger . . ."

"Fine."

We reached the eighth floor. I put my index finger to my lips and we stopped speaking. I walked alone to Davy's door. As I did this, I finally heard my father's voice: "*Adasciu, adasciu,* Ellissina, *furba!*" Carefully, carefully, be watchful. The same words he'd said to me when he floated in Agrigento's night sky. Either that or I was as bonkers as my half-sister.

The first thing I saw was neither human nor bird. The red leather armchair of my childhood – that familiar and beloved squat miniature of adult furniture – sat, almost illuminated, on the beige carpet between a chocolate-brown suede sofa and a large wooden writing desk. I made myself look away from it as quickly as possible, made myself look into the eyes of the person who most wanted to be seen.

"Hello, Petra."

"Hi, Ellissa. I told the guard I was you. Said I was Ellissa Major."

"I know. So I said I was Petra Major."

"You did? I like that. We are each other."

She seemed, if possible, even thinner. Her skin had a yellow-grey cast. The large blue eyes were still remarkable but she was blinking more quickly than I had remembered. Her clothes were the ones she'd been wearing when we met in Montréal – pale pink down-filled bomber jacket (far too heavy, a winter jacket), pink scarf and gloves. White jeans encased her stick-like legs, and white trainers had replaced the white Sorel boots. She was making a low grinding noise at the back of her throat, a steady gravelly hum, as she rocked slightly back and forth. The fingers of her left hand plucked at imaginary fluff on her scarf. Speeding, I thought, she's on some sort of stimulant.

She held a white wrought-iron birdcage in her right hand. In this cage, a cockatiel, not used to being held aloft in an unfamiliar environment, was nervously flying about. "I brought this bird for Davy. It is like an actor. You can teach it to say words. I named it Davy. When it is not so excited it can say 'pretty boy.'"

"That's wonderful, Petra. A perfect choice. Hello, Davy, no, don't get up. Stay where you are. You should take your break. Have your tea."

Petra almost growled. "Don't you want to hug each other? You love each other so much, yah?"

No, Davy, I thought. Don't move. Any sudden movement, any abrupt changes and this is going to escalate. "No. I have a terrible cold. Davy shouldn't come near me while he's working. I only came by . . ."

"Because you wanted your little girl chair?"

"No, actually. I have two tickets to the ballet tomorrow, and, with this cold, don't want to go. So, I was in the area and thought I'd give the tickets to Davy. He and Tariq could go. Have you met Tariq, Petra?"

"No. But I have seen him."

"Oh? Where?"

"At their flat in Bayswater. Coming and going. I watch. I watch my brother and his lover. They love each other too."

"You'd like Tariq, Petra. And he'd like you. He loves assemblage and sculpture. In fact, he knows your work. From one of your London shows."

"Yah? Is that true, Davy? Which one?"

"I'm not sure. A few years ago. There was an article in *Time Out*. He pointed out your name, Major, and wondered if we were related. I said yes, that you were my half-sister. That we did not really know each other, but that I wished we did. He went to the show. Said it was really good. I couldn't go because I was working, but he came home and praised it to me."

Through the clown makeup, as he talked, I could see light and understanding flooding Davy's film-ready face. That's right, Davy. She isn't just speedy and eccentric. She's filled with rage and drugs and she's barking mad. Stay on the sofa, my brother. And I should say something. Something about dinner. "Davy, you know, you should invite Petra to dinner. You, Tariq, Petra . . . and me."

"Yes, that's a great idea. When you're over that cold, we should all have dinner. At the flat. I'll cook. Or Tariq will. He's actually better at cooking than I am. Do you like Moroccan food, Petra?"

If she heard the question she ignored it. She was looking only at me. She bent her knees, still watching me, and put the white wrought-iron birdcage on the floor. The cockatiel fluttered about, then settled on his perch, eating birdseed that hung down in the shape of a bell. "Mama said you went to Daddy's funeral, in Italy, yah?"

"Yes. All of the Italian relatives were there. Only the Italians."

She pointed at Davy, her voice sharpening. "You did not go? I thought our father liked you. He, our father, says that you and Ellissa both work for your money. Me too, I work for my money, but this he does not care about. I work. Earn my own money. But this does not matter because I come out of a poisoned hole."

Davy started to raise a hand to his face, remembered the makeup and dropped it into the lap of his patched and faded denim overalls costume. His multicoloured striped jumper made me think of the rainbow in Gay Pride parades. I wondered if that had been Davy's idea. At some point in the future, if we had a future, I would ask him. Then I thought, of course we have a future. Stay calm, Ellissa. Talk to Petra. Dan is outside. Speak.

"Davy was filming this show, Petra. *Jimmy JollyJumper*. He could not leave London. I was the only one who went to Sicily." I do not mention Mammina, the woman who did her out of her share of the money. "I saw him. We spoke."

"You saw who?"

"Our father. He came to me in the night. In Agrigento. In Sicily. Maybe it was a dream but I don't think so. I believe he visited me. He asked about you. He said he was sorry."

"What do you mean?"

"We were talking. He was very angry with your mother. And with your sister. He said your mother was a bad wife. A liar and a thief . . ."

"Yah, liar! And pimp. A pimp of her daughter!"

"He asked, 'Do you see Petra?' I told him we'd had an argument. He said, 'Find her. Find Petra. Make up with her. She was not like the others. She is independent. She is an artist. Like your brother.'"

"He said that? I don't believe you."

"I swear. He said to find you. He said we are so few now, our family. I did not try to find you because I didn't think you would want to see me."

She held her place but lurched slightly, as if about to move closer. As I'd seen her do in Montréal, she clenched her hands into fists. She was looking at me so hard I thought her eyes would shatter like the blue glass eyes of dolls. "I will always want to see you, Ellissa. You are my sister."

She put her fingers over her upper lip, as I'd seen Floris do so many times. She did not say "Bad Petra." She just did Floris's gesture. Had she inherited it? Was Floris, like her mother, dead, with some grotesque bird dead nearby?

"Yes. Your sister. Forever."

She came to me. I held her. I knew that I could, as Pappino would say, "take her," but did not think it was the time. Or was I afraid of the violent chaos it would release? She broke from the embrace, and, still staring so hard, whispered, "What else? What else did he say?"

From somewhere, in the hope that truth would set me free, and because I was out of bluffs, I said, "He told me . . . he told me he liked being dead. It's never cold, he said. He was wearing this white night-shirt thing and he was barefoot and hovering in the dark starry sky and he said there were no fights in his new place and he was happy."

"What else? Did he say anything else?"

"He said he liked the flying."

"Yah. Everybody wants to fly."

BASTINA

It was so fast. People always say "It happened so fast." Actually, when you see it happen, it happens faster than that. The going is barely seen at all – an air-jostling movement, a flash of colours. What fills the room, what sustains, what I will see always, is the gone. The gone, with sky and clouds behind it.

Petra grabbed my childhood red leather chair, hurled it through the open window, and flew out after it. She thought she was half bird. A Storm Petrel. What bird watchers call "an accidental." I save animals. It's what I do. I've saved birds. I could not save Petra. She flew out and down. Straight down. Nine storeys.

Staring at the gone, I believed Petra's flight was my fault. I had just told her, a woman who thought she was a bird, I had told this bird-woman that our father – whose love she wanted enough to kill him for denying it to her – that he could fly. That I had seen him do this. And she spread her arms and tried to join him, to be with him where the rest of us could not follow. Not without first dying.

The gone became filled with people. Dan stood in front of me. He reached out. I backed away. He kept saying Liss, Liss, Liss. Davy's hand rested lightly on my shoulder. I heard people running up the stairs. They overwhelmed the room, saying all these names, all names for me. All the hissy esses. Liss, Lissa, Ellissa. The guard from downstairs, said 'Missus Major.' There were other words, transformed into Petra's speedy buzzing, amplified. A thousand bees. The loudest buzz, the loudest name, came from someone who was not in the room.

I'd heard the name since the day I was born.

Ellissina. No, I thought. No. My name is Bastina. I am called Bastina because. Sometimes I must. Just. Stop.

AFTER: A GOOD DRUMMER

County Galway, Ireland – 2003

I sold the Southwold Animal Clinic to Betty for less than she wanted to give and more than I wanted to take. She simply refused to accept "a free gift. Not after all your years of work, Ellissa."

In truth, she'd worked alongside me from the beginning. Further, she'd done almost everything at the clinic from the start of Papp's Montréal heart attack. Animal owners who'd once believed their pets could only be comfortable with me always learned to know and trust Betty. Her talent for ministering to beasties was superlative. She and her veterinarily gifted young niece are in charge there now.

She wished to remain in her own house just up the road, having lived there for twenty-two years. Samantha, her niece, yearning for a locally respectable way to live on her own, happily moved into my little house, where her parents, and anyone else in the small community, could keep a watchful eye on her. I still own the house, and have both my own room (Papp's old room) and run of the place when in residence. I'll be in residence for at least two summer months a year, so Bet can have her holiday-time.

In leaving Southwold I freed Dan from a relationship that would never give him the love he needed and deserved. There were at least three Southwolders waiting and wanting to give him that love.

I now live with Helena (my father's third wife) and her husband, Dr. Jim Finnerty, in County Galway. Jim cares for large animals (horses, cattle, sheep – mostly horses. The west of Ireland is horse country). I'm Jim's new business partner – the small animal vet at the Galway Bay Animal Clinic. I'll be open for business in about a month, and have been taking tea with local animals and their humans. All species have been gracious and welcoming, with the exception of a twitchy, growly teacup poodle in a diamond collar. I think the collar may be the dog's problem. I know the collar is *my* problem, but believe the dog and his owner are moving to California to do something in what Diamond Lady calls "the film industry."

Davy has spent a weekend here. There was a lot of music, beer and laughter, though Davy would not, "under any circs," ride a horse ("If I broke anything, the Jimmy Jollies would sue me blind. It's in me contract!"). He and Tariq will visit us together soon. In fact, Tariq and Helena have already spoken – something about "nubby silk in a pale lemon colour."

Christmas will be, as always, with Mammina in Sicily, and now with the Maggiore crew as well. Liddru is quite old. I want to see him again.

Mammina is not terribly interested in Ireland, though she will visit at some point, if only to have a look at "Vanni's Irish." Helena knows you can't fight with someone who isn't angry with you. It will be fine. Intense but fine. And I can visit with Mammina when she is in London for Cognoscenti or real-estate business. She is an amazing woman, and went fiercely through a swamp for all our sakes. Hugs or no, we love each other.

Every weekend afternoon that our schedules permit, just before sunset, Helena, Jim and I ride together along the beach, as I used to do with Helena and my father, when we'd ride to Connemara to see the wild ponies. The ponies, or their children, are still running free – but only free to go round and round. They are glorious creatures but do not have many choices. They don't seem to need them. People do. I think we do.

Helena's Irish Setter hair is now mostly silver or naturally blonde (this, apparently, happens to some redheads; they go blonde and then the blonde turns silver) with stripy strands of Sienna orange.

Jim is tall and skinny – Bony Mahoney, Helena calls him. He has white hair, a black and grey moustache, a long nose with a bump in the middle and a two-dimpled smile that lights a room and welcomes a guest.

They sold the two racehorses that Papp left to Helena. "It wouldn't have been fair to keep them. They are thoroughbreds and need to be exercised and raced. And the sale has paid for repairs on both the house and the clinic, plus needed equipment."

From my room in our little house (still called "The Weaver's House"), I can see Galway Bay.

Every night, after dinner and before sleep, at Helena's suggestion, I write in this journal. I began it with my childhood, but that may change. Helena, who keeps a journal, says to just write what comes, as it comes – it can be put in order later. I think a lot about Petra. I know, from Petra and me, from both my parents, and from the animals who are my work, that both love given and love withdrawn can make a creature go savage.

Writing, sometimes just a few lines; other times through the night until sun-up, helps me to be less afraid of whatever I may come to understand. It is re-opening all the love, all the craziness, the sudden surprises, the twists and turns – all the surreality that has been so much a part of my life. So I write. And, to my surprise, I also sing.

Jim Finnerty, Large Animal Veterinarian, is also the drummer for *Off the Leash and Out Loose*, a Galway garage band comprised of four veterinarians and a bass-playing jockey. I am their Chick Singer – Blues, Jazz and Sloppy Woppy Classics.

Helena says it's time to let go of Bastina. She says Bastina protected a child but that I can now protect myself. Without what she calls "The living death, the long inbreath" of "just stopping." She also says I can stop thinking about pleasing my father and just sing what I like. I have assured her that I've loved singing Sloppy Woppy all my life – that it's in my blood.

I'm not trying to contact Papp any more. If he needs me he'll find me. My seeking him tangles up his spirit. And mine. So says Helena, who is quite unscornfully smart about such things.

As I write my life, from the beginning to now, Jim says it's about "playing through the pain." That's a drum thing. When you play drums, there comes a point where you feel like your wrists are going to fall off. The pain shoots up your arms and into your brain. A good drummer, who keeps playing through the pain, will come to the other side of that pain . . . and be able to play all night.

I want very much to be a good drummer.

ACKNOWLEDGEMENTS

This book was begun at the Baltic Centre for Writers and Translators in Visby, Gotland, Sweden.

Work continued at Waves of Three Seas in Rhodes, Greece.

The first draft was completed in Shakespeare Room at the Hawthornden Castle Writers and Translators Retreat in Lasswade, Midlothian, Scotland.

Subsequent drafts were written or edited at Toronto Writers' Centre, Gibraltar Point (Toronto Island), Garden Court Hotel (London, UK) and in two small live/work studios in Toronto, Canada, and Visby, Sweden.

To first-readers Martin Sherman, Tom St. Louis, and Marc Côté for taking time from their own work to give me invaluable input and guidance.

To the Ontario Arts Council and Exile Editions for a Writers' Reserve Grant.

To Toronto Wordstage for *Savage Adoration*'s first public reading.

To Mrs. Valeria Sestieri Lee, long-time professor at the University of Calgary (ret.), for vetting the Italian used in the book.

To funeral directors Richard Paul and Alan Cole.

To veterinarians John Reeve-Newson (Canada) and Gareth Braine (UK).

To caninophile and veterinary resource, the Hon. Simon Callow, CBE.

To the website of the Royal Veterinary College, UK.

To the National Library of Scotland, Edinburgh, and the Almedalen University Library, Visby, Sweden, for veterinary and avian resource books and gracious personal assistance.

To my literary representative, Peter William Taylor.

To my literary and copy editor, poet and author Priscila Uppal, for commitment, enthusiasm, incisive notes, and helping to balance the who and the what.

To Samantha Vite for personifying Ellissa Major on this book's cover, and to first-rate photographer, Mark Tearle, for perfectly capturing her personification.

To Cylla von Tiedemann, for, as always, capturing the part of my soul that belongs to the story.

To Meaghan Strimas, for proofreading the final text with the skill and literary engagement of an editor.

To Patrik Muskos of Baltic Centre, for technical assistance above and beyond the call.

To Exile Editions and *Exile: The Literary Quarterly*, publisher and art-director Michael Callaghan, uber-proofer Nina Callaghan, and particularly founder and Editor-in-chief, Barry Callaghan, for long-time belief in and support for my work.

To all these, my heartfelt appreciation and thanks.

Gale Zoë Garnett
Toronto, Canada

This book is entirely printed on FSC certified paper.